"**Y**ou know the forms well enough and stand pretty with a sword, but you've never fought for blood, have you, lass?"

Jill could only shake her head—no, she'd never fought for blood. Not real blood. Only ranks, medals, and maybe a college scholarship.

"What's your name, lass?"

"Jill. Jill Archer," she said, her voice scratching. She only just noticed that she was thirsty.

"And, Jill, how do you come to be adrift in the wide sea so far from home?"

The tears almost broke then, and she took a moment to answer. "I don't know."

Also by
CARRIE VAUGHN

Voices of Dragons

CARRIE VAUGHN

Steel

HARPER TEEN
An Imprint of HarperCollins*Publishers*

HarperTeen is an imprint of HarperCollins Publishers.

Steel
Copyright © 2011 by Carrie Vaughn, LLC.
All rights reserved. Printed in the United States of America.
No part of this book may be used or reproduced in any manner whatsoever without written
permission except in the case of brief quotations embodied in critical articles and reviews. For
information address HarperCollins Children's Books, a division of HarperCollins Publishers,
10 East 53rd Street, New York, NY 10022.
www.epicreads.com

Library of Congress Cataloging-in-Publication Data
Vaughn, Carrie.
    Steel / Carrie Vaughn. — 1st ed.
        p.   cm.
    Summary: When Jill, a competitive high school fencer, goes with her family on vacation
to the Bahamas, she is magically transported to an early eighteenth-century pirate ship in the
middle of the ocean.
    ISBN 978-0-06-195650-8
    [1. Time travel—Fiction.   2. Pirates—Fiction.   3. Fencing—Fiction.   4. Caribbean
area—History—18th century—Fiction.]   I. Title.
PZ7.V462St   2011   2010012631
[Fic]—dc22   CIP
                                                                                              AC

Typography by Amy Ryan
12 13 14 15 16   CG/BV   10 9 8 7 6 5 4 3 2 1
❖
First paperback edition, 2012

To my family

Steel

1

EN GARDE

Jill shook her legs out one at a time. Rolled her shoulders. Loosened up. Rearranged her hold on her weapon once again, curling gloved fingers around the grip. It nestled into her hand like it had been molded there, the épée blade becoming an extension of her arm.

Across from her, on a long, five-foot-wide strip of combat, stood her opponent, a tall, powerful-limbed girl in a bleach-white fencing jacket who seemed more like a linebacker than a fencer. Her face was a shadow behind the mesh of her mask. Jill bounced in place, flicking her épée so it whipped against the air, as if she couldn't wait to start.

The score was tied. This was the last point. The air seemed to have gone out of the room, a cavernous gymnasium where two dozen fencing strips had held competitors fighting and winning and losing all day. Only a few fencers remained now. The winner of this bout would get third place for the tournament. Bronze medal. The loser, fourth place, and nothing else. A pat on the back. And Jill needed this win to qualify for the Junior World Fencing Championships. This was her last chance.

Let it all go, Jill told herself. It was just another tournament, one of hundreds she'd fenced in. Let her muscles do what they knew how to do. Remember why she loved this: With a few flicks of her sword she would outwit her enemy, and even through the mesh of the mask, Jill would see the startled look on the girl's shadowed face when she scored a touch on her.

The official glanced between them, judging their readiness. *"En garde."*

Let it go, do your job.

"Allez!"

Épées raised, they approached, step by careful step. Jill knew her opponent, a girl from Texas, was cautious, but when she finally committed herself she'd be strong. She'd plow Jill over if she could, sending her into a panic, and score the point before anyone could blink. So Jill wanted to strike first, before her opponent had a chance to gather herself.

Arm outstretched, Jill feinted high, wagging her blade up in a move that looked like it would strike her opponent's mask, her footwork carrying her too fast to back out of the commitment. As she hoped, the Texas girl lifted her sword to parry, exposing her legs and the lower half of her torso— all targets waiting for a good, clean hit.

But the parry itself was a feint, and the Texan was ready for her. When Jill circled her blade to avoid the parry, the other blade circled with her, blocking her intended target, knocking her out of the way—leaving Jill exposed. Quickly—now she was the one in a panic—she scrambled back in a retreat and yanked her blade up to parry.

Steel struck steel, moving too fast for Jill to feel it much. Her hand was already turning the sword to its next motion, to counter the Texan's concerted attack.

Jill pulled it together. Kept her focus on the job at hand.

Her mind seemed to fade as her body moved by instinct, and it felt wonderful. Her motions flowed, her steps were easy—she could almost see where the Texas girl's épée prepared to strike. Then, she saw her opening. Her opponent kept attacking low, trying to sneak under Jill's defense. All Jill had to do was use that pattern against her. Wait for the next low attack, sweep up, strike home as the Texan's sword was also extending toward her—

A buzzer rang, the signal from the electronic scoring box.

Buttons on the tips of the épées recorded hits. Signals traveled from the button along a wire nested in the blade to the back of the guard, then through cords laced up the sleeve and out behind the jacket to plug into the scoring box. Often, the movements happened so quickly, the touches from the other sword were so light you couldn't feel them. The lights on the box told the truth.

Jill had hit the Texan, she knew she had, right on her breastbone. She'd felt the pressure through her hand and arm. But her opponent's sword had slipped inside her defenses as well. Jill looked at the lights—her opponent's red light buzzed brightly. Jill's light should have been green—but it was dark. She had hit a fraction of a second after her opponent had killed her. Her point didn't count.

Last touch and the bout went to the other fighter. The referee called it. There was cheering.

Jill stood dazed a moment, breathing hard, still locked in the fight, her muscles lost in instinct, waiting for the next attack to come. The Texan pulled off her mask and tucked it under her arm. She had a round face with strong eyebrows, dark eyes, and black hair tied in a long braid. She didn't look pleased that she'd won—no smiles, no flush of victory. No, she looked smug. Like she hadn't expected any other outcome.

Slowly, Jill took off her own mask, shook out her short, dark hair, turned her sword away, and stepped forward to take the winner's hand. She had to be polite. Had to be a good sport.

Her fingers fumbled, trying to unplug her body cord from the socket behind her.

Coach Martin, a honey-haired thirtysomething woman who'd fenced in the Olympics back in the day, took the plug away from her and detached it. Smiling, she patted Jill on the shoulder. Jill still didn't feel anything.

"It was a good bout. You did fine," Coach Martin said.

All Jill could think was, half a second too slow. That was all it took.

Habit more than anything guided Jill through putting her gear away: Wipe down her weapons, roll up her body cords, track down her gloves, fold up her jacket and white knickers, and put them along with her mask and the rest in her bag. In the locker room, she showered, though for not as long as she'd have liked because there wasn't any hot water left. She dried her hair without looking in the mirror. The bout with the Texan had been the last of the day, and Jill had daw-dled—which meant she had the locker room to herself. She didn't have to face anyone and try to smile like a good sport.

When she came out of the locker room, she looked like a normal kid again, in loafers, jeans, and a sweater, bag over her shoulder, scuffing her feet as she walked. Her secret identity—Jill the amazing swordswoman—was packed safely away. After today she wasn't sure her secret identity was all that amazing. She was just another kid fencer who wasn't going to the championships.

Just like the locker room, the lobby of the arena had cleared out. A few volunteers and officials were taking down signs, but the competitors, coaches, and families had all gone. Only Jill's entourage remained, waiting for her: Coach Martin, along with her parents. The coach said something to the couple, then stepped forward to meet Jill, who must have looked particularly dejected, because Martin put her arm around her shoulders.

"Jill, you did fine out there. You did great. The competition was tough. Really tough."

Standard pep talk. Sometimes it made Jill feel better; this one just sounded like platitudes. "I wasn't good enough to qualify."

"You can try again next year," said Coach Martin. "And in a couple of years you can try for the Olympics. You're good enough for that. You're one of the best épéeists in the world for your age group."

But when it counted, when it all came down to one touch,

Jill had been half a second too slow. How close had it been, really? What if she missed qualifying for the Olympics by half a second? She'd come in fourth in a national tournament. She ought to be celebrating, but she felt like she'd been hollowed out.

"Well, how about it? Ready to take on the Olympics?"

"I don't know," Jill said. She wasn't thinking much beyond the next five minutes and getting back home.

Martin patted her shoulder and turned to walk with her to her parents. "Come on, kid. This wasn't your day, but the next day will be."

Her parents were smiling.

"I'm so proud of you, Jill." Her mother came forward to wrap her up in a big hug, like Jill was still a little girl, even though Jill stood three inches taller than her now. Dad patted her on the shoulder. Jill tried to smile back, but it was hard, and they noticed. It made them even more enthusiastic. They'd always been supportive, shuttled her back and forth to practices, funded her without complaint, and it made her want to win even more. She sometimes wondered if they were hiding disappointment when she didn't win.

And sometimes she wondered if maybe the pep talks were wrong—maybe, no matter how hard she worked, she just wasn't good enough.

2
RETREAT

Lying in a hammock tied between two palm trees, a closed book in her hands, Jill thought about Errol Flynn. And Zorro, and lightsabers, and what it would be like to fight from the rigging of a sailing ship. Really, though, she was still thinking about that slow half a second and fourth place.

She could still feel the moment, staring down her opponent, the weight of her épée pulling at her hand, her arms and legs itching to move. She only fought for electronic points, but she could imagine she was some blazing hero. But the hero wasn't supposed to lose by half a second. She'd been afraid to tell Coach Martin that she did want to compete in the Olympics—the modern equivalent of battling pirates on the high main, as she saw it. But what if she got close and missed, like she had in the tournament? How empty would she feel, then? What if, after all was said and done, she just wasn't good enough?

A mild sea breeze blew. The palm trees creaked and the hammock swayed, just a little, reminding Jill that she was supposed to be relaxing. A month after the tournament, the family—Jill, her parents, younger brother, and even younger sister—was in the Bahamas for spring break. Their plane landed two days ago in the middle of the afternoon, and when they emerged into the open, the sun blazed, and Jill squinted and ducked away like a mouse creeping out of a dark hole. Her parents rented a car in the colorful town of Nassau with its old forts, sparkling resort hotels, and rows of cruise ships; then they drove the family out to a tropical village and a vacation house they'd rented for the week. Beach, sun, swimming, snorkeling, golf, hiking, and all the rest.

But Jill had spent almost two days now lying on the hammock, pretending to read, and thinking too much. She'd only been to practice a couple of times since the tournament—usually, she went nearly every day. Coach Martin said it was fine to take a little time off, and they'd talk about a new training schedule when she got back from the trip.

That would be in a week, and Jill would have to have an answer. Did she want to keep going? Try again next year, like Coach Martin had said? Go back to practicing every day—so she could come in fourth? But it wasn't about winning, or the medals, or all that. All the familiar clichés. She was supposed to be doing this because she loved it. She had to keep reminding herself.

"Jill!" her mother called from the house. "We're going to the beach, don't you want to come?"

Sighing, Jill squinted at scattered beams of sunlight shining through palm fronds. "Not really."

The next time Jill's mother spoke, she was standing at the house's back doorway, shading her eyes and looking out. Slathered in sunscreen, she had on her one-piece swimsuit, a towel wrapped around her waist, and flip-flops on her feet. She already had a tan and seemed to be enjoying herself.

"Jill, this is a family vacation. Come to the beach with us. You can bring your book."

"I don't really feel like it."

Mom put her hands on her hips, and her brow furrowed. Her "concerned" face. "What's wrong?"

It would have been easy to say nothing. Jill shook her head. "I should have won that bout."

"You're still on about that? You'll win next time."

"But what if I don't?"

"Jill, don't worry about it, you're supposed to be on vacation. Now come on."

Clearly, her mother wasn't going to let her mope at will. Giving in was easier than arguing at the moment. Jill went.

The bright sun, soothing white beaches, and picture-perfect views of palm trees and bright blue ocean didn't do much for Jill's mood. Gray skies would have suited her better. But she tried to make a good showing, for her mother's sake: lying on a towel on the beach while eight-year-old Mandy and ten-year-old Tom ran around screaming, splashing in and out of the waves. Her siblings kept yelling at her to join them, that the water was warm and she should try snorkeling, it was so clear and they could see rocks and fish and shells and *everything*. At least they were having a good time. Mandy hadn't stopped talking since they arrived, going on and on about sharks and seashells and where they should go looking for pirate treasure. That was after the visit to the Pirates Museum in Nassau. Apparently, the island had been covered with pirates some three hundred years ago. Jill kept telling her that all the pirate treasure had been found a long time ago, and real pirates didn't bury treasure anyway. Mandy didn't care; she was still going to talk about it.

Jill hadn't even put on her swimsuit, but wore a tank top and clamdiggers. Her one concession was going barefoot, and she dug her toes in the warm sand.

Her father had gone to play golf. Her mother stretched out on a lounge chair beside her, sipping from a fruity drink with a paper umbrella and a pineapple rind sticking out of it. Jill had asked for a taste, and her mother had refused. "It's got rum in it," she'd said.

Maybe the trip would be more fun if Jill were old enough to drink.

Reading in the sun, even wearing sunglasses, gave her a headache, so she set the book aside and tried to take a nap. Then she gave up on the nap and stood. "I'm going to take a walk."

Her mother blinked awake—*she'd* managed a nap. "Where to?"

"Just down the beach," she said. "I'll go for a while and turn around and come back."

For a moment, her mother looked like she might argue. But she didn't. "All right. Be careful."

Jill started walking.

The beach wasn't crowded, but it wasn't empty, which she would have preferred. Lots of families seemed to be on vacation, as well as couples of every age. People, greasy with sunscreen, lay on towels and baked on the sand. Some played volleyball. Some, like her, walked barefoot on wet sand, at the edge of where the waves reached. She kept going, past the people, to where the more attractive, sandy portion of the beach narrowed, and palm trees grew almost to the water. Voices fell away, drowned out by the sound of waves. She kept walking.

She could understand how someone could lose herself, walking along a beach. It was meditative: the roll of the waves, the repetitive movement of water and patterns of froth that traveled back and forth along the sand were constant, along with the noise—the rush, splash, echo of always-moving water. Beautiful, entrancing. It never changed—but at the same time the pattern the breaking waves made was always different, and she could just keep watching it. The waves, the surf, and the ocean that went on to a flat horizon.

Walking in sand was a lot of work. Her feet dug in, slipping a little with every step. Her legs had to push harder. This was a good workout. Then again, she was probably moving faster than she needed to. You were supposed to just stroll along a beach, not march. She didn't care. She didn't mind sweating.

She could just keep walking, never go back. She could turn into a beach bum and never make another decision about what to do next. The idea sounded enticing.

When her bare toe scuffed against something hard in the sand, she stopped. It was too heavy to be a shell. Maybe a stone. She knelt and brushed the sand away, feeling for the object her foot had discovered.

It was a slender length of rusted steel, flat, about six inches long and a half an inch wide. It tapered to a point at one end and was jagged at the other, as if it had broken. A thousand people would step over it and think it trash, but not her.

This was the tip of a rapier, the solid shape of a real sword. The original source of the modern, flimsy weapons she fenced with. Every fencing book she'd ever seen had a picture of rapiers like that, to show where the sport came from. This tip must have broken off and might have been rusting in the ocean for centuries, waves pushing it along the sandy bottom until it washed up here. Dark brown flakes came off in her hand. The edges were dull enough that she ran her finger along them without harm—though her skin tingled when she thought about what the piece of steel represented. Was it a pirate sword? Had it broken in a duel? In a battle? Maybe it had fallen from a ship. Looking around, she studied the sand as if the rest of the sword might be lying nearby. She imagined a long, powerful rapier with an intricate swept hilt, like something from a museum or a movie. An Errol Flynn movie. But that was stupid. The tip had broken, and it would have washed away from the rest of the sword a long time ago.

Maybe there was a sword in a museum somewhere, missing six inches. Maybe she should tell someone about this.

Maybe the pirate museum in Nassau would want it.

But it was just a broken, rusted piece of steel. What were the odds that someone strolling along the beach would find it and recognize what it was, like she did? No one would want it, really. No one would miss it.

She didn't know how far she'd come or how long she'd been walking, but she'd left behind signs of civilization. She couldn't see any roads or hear any vehicles. No boats were visible out on the water, and there weren't any people. Just blowing palm trees, a strip of sand, and the endless waves. She might as well have been on a desert island. Which made her feel strangely peaceful. Being the only person on an island, looking out at the ocean? Maybe you'd go crazy. Or you might think that you'd finally found some peace and quiet. No pressure on a desert island.

At least walking along the shore she couldn't possibly get lost. She turned around and started back. Before she came within sight of the first people and buildings, she slipped the broken rapier tip in her pocket.

It was weird; she felt like she had something she shouldn't, as if she'd stolen something. But she'd found it; she hadn't taken it from anyone. Maybe she blushed because she liked knowing something no one else did. She liked having a little bit of secret treasure.

3

DISENGAGE

Her mother was very into the idea of togetherness. "Jill, you're going to go away to college in a couple of years. Who knows what'll happen after that? This may be our last big family trip together and I want us to spend as much time together as we can."

No pressure or anything.

The day after the beach, Mom planned a boat tour.

"What kind of boat?" Tom kept asking as Mom herded them all into the rental car.

"Will it have sails?" Mandy said.

"Or cannons?" Tom asked.

"No cannons," their mother said. "It's just a tour boat; it goes up and down the coast and that's it."

Jill's silence was a contrast to the laughing and joking of the others. She wasn't encouraged when they arrived at the dock and a banner hanging on the side of the office announced: PARTY CRUISES. The sign showed lots of cartoon pictures of parrots with eye patches holding margaritas in clawed feet. Scratchy reggae music played through speakers. Now Jill was going to be trapped on a boat full of people having more fun than she was.

She hung back and kept her hands in the pockets of her clamdiggers, fingers brushing the rusted piece of rapier she'd brought with her. Last night, she'd put it on the windowsill next to her bed. She didn't want to leave it alone, as if it might start speaking, whispering cryptic and important secrets, and she had to be there to hear it. Maybe it would be a good luck charm.

The tour company did, in fact, have sailing ships with cannons—fake ships that ran on motors, with fake masts and sails and plastic cannons. The boat for their tour was more mundane, thirty or forty feet long with a cabin toward the front, a clean white hull, a big motor, and plastic cushions on the seats around the outside. Very modern. The oily smell of diesel overcame the salt smell of the ocean.

A dozen people had signed up for the tour, and a dockhand guided them onto the back of the boat—and he yelled at Tom and Mandy to stop running. Jill found a place to sit toward the back and looked over the water through her sunglasses.

Dad picked a place next to her on the boat. The first day on the island he'd forgotten to use sunscreen and had a sunburn that was already peeling across his nose and cheeks. That didn't keep him from smiling. Today, he had on a sheen of sunscreen and was wearing a wide-brimmed hat that shaded his whole face. He also wore a plaid cotton shirt and looked every bit the tourist.

"This ought to be fun," he said, striking up a conversation.

"Yeah," Jill said, noncommittal, looking out at the water.

"Mom says you're still upset about the tournament." He'd just glanced at her mother, who must have put him up to this. Jill could almost hear her saying, *You try talking to her. . . .*

Jill shrugged. "I don't know. I can't stop thinking about it. It was so close."

"There'll be other tournaments."

"That's kind of the problem."

"Ah. Your mom and I—I hope you've never felt like we've pushed you, or put too much pressure on you."

"No," Jill said, shaking her head. "No, this is all me. It's just—I'm disappointed, and everyone else must be disappointed. I was so close."

"I guess if I said, 'Winning isn't everything,' you'd give me one of those looks, wouldn't you?" he said.

And she gave him one of those looks, but tried to turn it into a smile. She probably just ended up looking confused.

"Well," he said. "Try to forget about it for a little while, at least. Try to enjoy yourself."

Mandy and Tom were now leaning over the side, trying to reach into the water, and Mom was pulling them back to their seats. Jill was suddenly jealous of them.

After twenty more minutes of waiting for people to settle, the boat motored away from the dock, chugging and trailing wisps of black smoke, which seemed ironic, considering they were supposed to be enjoying the pristine scenery. Tom and Mandy may actually have been right—sails and wind seemed more suited to boating in a tropical paradise.

Once on the water, the waves hardly rocked them. They traveled smoothly while the tour guide told them stories.

The guide was a beach bum–looking guy, skin tanned like leather, white hair rough and windblown, stubble for a beard. He looked ancient but seemed younger in the quickness of his movements and the brightness in his voice. Sitting near the cabin, the PA microphone in one hand, he gestured widely, pointing vaguely toward the island or out to sea as he talked about the old weathered forts overlooking the harbor, naval battles between the British and Spanish, and what pirates did to capture merchant ships. More pirate stories. Legends such as Blackbeard had found a haven here. They lived reckless, lawless lives. The words condemned the pirate culture, but the guide had a gleam in his eye.

"So is there buried treasure on the island?" Tom asked.

"Contrary to all the stories, pirates didn't bury their treasure, lad," the guide said kindly. Just like Jill had told him. "Most of them spent it all before they'd ever have a chance to bury it. They'd come to shore and go straight to the tavern. Not much has changed, eh?" A few of the passengers chuckled.

Tom looked disappointed, and the guide continued. "Sometimes people find gold doubloons or other things washed up on the beach. A lot of ships wrecked between here and Florida. That's where the real treasure is."

Jill touched the rapier point in her pocket, still feeling like she'd stolen something precious.

"Now, a lot of people ask me, why are pirates so fascinating? They were vicious criminals, weren't they? They robbed and murdered, didn't they? The modern pirates out in Somalia sure aren't heroes. So why do we make these pirates into heroes? I say it's because they were free in a time when not many people were. Did you know pirate ships were some of the first democracies? Crews voted on their captains. A good captain had to listen to his crew, and the ship was only as good as the crew. A good crew was a family. There's something admirable in that."

It all seemed unreal to Jill, remembering the shore that was crowded with hotels and the harbor that was filled with sleek white sailboats and massive cruise ships.

"Are there any ghosts on the island?" Mandy said.

The guide launched into more stories about pirate ghosts and ghostly cannons firing from Fort Charlotte at midnight.

Jill sat close to the edge, her arm over the side, turning her face to the wind and letting the sea spray touch her. The coast continued to look like a postcard—white sand, palm trees, and amazing blue water. She gave up on thinking about her life and let her mind wander. There was something about the way the sunlight played on the water. She could even ignore her siblings.

Once they'd passed a certain point, leaving the sheltered part of the coast, the sea became rougher. Jill found herself holding on to the side with both hands as the ship rose and fell, rocking and slapping against the waves, which seemed larger than they had at the start of the cruise. A few people cried out as they lost their balance, then laughed it off. Tom and Mandy seemed to think it was huge fun. The wind blew Jill's hair into her face; she brushed it away.

They were supposed to be having lunch at noon. The crew had already pulled out a box full of sandwiches and a cooler that they said was full of rum punch. Jill didn't bother asking her mother if she could have any. But they paused; white clouds that had gathered picturesquely on the horizon all morning were darkening. Gray streaks from cloud to ocean showed rain. They'd traveled farther out to sea—the island was a rough smudge behind them, a crowd of foliage, no details visible. The laughter turned nervous—but they couldn't be heading into a storm, because a tour boat would never do that. Right?

Now this was exciting.

"Everyone take a seat," the guide said. "We'll be through this in a moment. And if you feel like heaving ho, do it over the side, okay?"

Most of passengers chuckled, but a few of them sat quickly on cushions around the sides, just in case.

"Jill? Jill, where are you?" Jill's mother called from the other side of the cabin. Mom was herding the kids; Jill recognized the tone of voice. She stood and turned toward the front of the boat to answer.

A large wave surged under them then, sending the boat rocking steeply. Jill, the world-class athlete who'd never yet lost her balance in a fencing bout, fell. Stumbling back, she hit the side of the boat and went over. Grabbing uselessly for the edge, she rolled into the ocean. Her father shouted, scrambling to his feet. She saw his arms reaching for her as she went under.

From dry land, the ocean looked so calm, peaceful. Serene blue waters. All that great scenery the adults talked about. From underwater, it was chaos. Waves pitched her, her sunglasses were torn away, the water was cold, shocking after the tropical air. She couldn't catch her breath—swallowed water instead. Flailing, she searched for up, groped for the surface—couldn't find it. Her lungs were tightening. It had been sunny a moment ago—where was the sun?

Someone grabbed her. Hands twisted into her clothing and pulled her into the air. She clutched at her rescuers, gasped for air, heaving deep breaths that tasted of brine, slimy and salty. But she was out of the water. She was safe. She wasn't going to die.

She landed hard on an unsteady wooden surface. The hands let her go, and she grabbed for some kind of hold to steady herself against the rocking of the waves.

Scrubbing water from her face, she opened her eyes and looked.

She expected to see the tour boat. But this boat was too small, almost a rowboat, with two sets of oars. Bottom and sides of plain wood, not polished fiberglass. No motor grumbled. And what should have been a clear stretch of ocean was filled with debris—broken wood, barrels bobbing along the waves, tangles of rope and canvas floating on the water. Something had been smashed to pieces here. A faint scent of burning touched the air.

Then there were the people.

Inside the rowboat, five men surrounded her, one bald, the others with long, greasy hair tied back. The ones without full beards still looked like they hadn't shaved in days. A couple had gold rings in their ears. One had a ring in his nose, through the middle. They wore rough shirts and loose trousers, and went barefoot.

They'd started rowing the little boat to a ship a few hundred feet away. A long, two-masted sailing ship, sails furled, riding the waves, up and down.

Jill had seen some of the other party boats that advertised as pirate ships, with their tall masts, rippling canvas sails, and skull-and-crossbones flags. This must have been one of those, with a particularly enthusiastic crew. Maybe it was a theme party with costumes. She'd fallen out of the tour boat, and these guys came along and picked her up. Maybe they'd let her have some of the rum punch. But that didn't explain the wreckage in the water. She didn't think she'd been in the water that long. Maybe a minute. On the other hand, maybe it had been longer—she felt like she had almost drowned. Could she have drifted that far from the tour boat in that time?

When she leaned on the edge of the rowboat to look for the tour boat her family was on, she couldn't see anything. No other vessel was in sight. The shore of the island was even farther away—a gray haze, that was all. Maybe the tour boat was behind the pirate party ship. The sky over them was scattered with clouds, thin, dissipating in a brisk wind, as if the threatening storm had ended.

The men on the rowboat weren't smiling, and didn't look like they'd come from any party.

Jill stayed alone in the middle of the boat, gripping the sides, while four of the men rowed. The fifth, the bald one, glared at her but didn't say a word. None of them even looked at her, just a piece of flotsam they'd picked out of the water.

"What's happening?" she asked, her voice shaking. She tried to sound braver. "Who are you guys?"

They didn't answer.

The boat was coming alongside the larger vessel, with its wide, sloping hull, two tall masts, and collection of triangular sails. Maybe she could ask someone there what this was all about, and they could take her back to the island.

The bald man shouted orders, a few monosyllabic calls

that Jill didn't understand, and ropes came down from the deck of the ship. She expected to see some kind of ladder, some easy way for them to climb on board—then there'd be a radio or something the captain could use to call the tour bout.

The men in the rowboat got to work tying ropes to cleats. The ropes looped over struts attached perpendicularly to the masts. Men on deck started pulling, ropes started creaking, and the rowboat lifted out of the water.

The rest of the men were climbing up the hull of the larger ship as lengths of rope were passed down to them. Instead of a ladder there were thin wooden slats nailed into the hull to use as toe holds. Not very helpful, Jill thought.

The bald man handed the end of a rope to her. "Climb," he ordered.

Was he kidding? She didn't know if she could, but she thought she'd better try. She watched the others expertly pull themselves up, hand over hand, using their feet to balance against the hull. Under other circumstances—like if this really was a party boat and she was supposed to be here—she might have had fun with it. But everything about the situation was wrong. Nobody checked to see if she was okay, and nobody was smiling.

She gripped the rope and started climbing.

The climb took forever, it seemed. She was shaking from

the shock of falling in the water, and her muscles felt like rubber—too soft, too stretchy, like they did after a full day of fencing. And she didn't know what was going to happen when she reached the deck of the ship. But she climbed, slowly, one step at a time, remembering to breathe.

The bald man rode in the rowboat as it was hauled up the side.

Finally, she reached the side—made of plain, weathered wood, like the rowboat. She hooked her arms over it, managed to swing one leg up, then rolled onto the new ship. She sprawled out on the deck.

The boards under her smelled like mildew, rotten with salt and damp that was never going to go away. There were cannons on wheels lined up along the side and lashed into place. The ship creaked—wood bending, ropes twisting, waves lapping against the hull. She heard this because all else was silent. The deck was filled with people, all shapes, sizes, colors. All men. And all of them looked angry. Or hungry. They were all staring at her. They'd left a space open around her, but in a second they could close that space, they could close in on *her*. When they pressed forward, she could feel their steps under her hands, where she crouched on the deck. She stood clumsily.

"Guess the salvage wasn't a waste after all," one of them said.

"Not at all, we found ourselves a nice bit of cargo," said the bald man, and the rest laughed. They leered with rotten and gap-toothed grins.

"She's a bit skinny, in't she?" This one poked at her, pinching the flesh of her forearm. She slapped at his hand and lurched away, but another set of hands were there, grabbing at her. This only made them laugh more.

This wasn't a party boat. This was something else.

Whoever these people were, whatever was happening, they held their bodies like predators ready to strike, and their gazes showed wicked, murderous desire. She felt lightheaded.

Thinking she'd be better off jumping right back into the water, she glanced behind her. A couple of the men had moved along the side, blocking her escape that way. So she was stuck. Trapped. *Screwed.*

Except that she recognized something else in the situation: Several of the men carried swords with long, slender blades. Rapiers. Besides the cannons on deck she didn't see any more serious weapons. Nothing like handguns. Only long knives. She understood rapiers. Jill could make a feint. Show them she wasn't easy pickings. It might even work.

Swinging back, she made toward the side, as if she planned to shove past the men and dive over in a spectacular and stupid bid to escape. A shout went up, and as she hoped, the men behind her reached out, grabbing at her to hold her back and keep her from jumping. She'd noted which one of them had a rapier—he kept it down, out of the way so as not to impale anyone while they hauled her from the side. Having misdirected them, she dug her shoulder into this one's chest, ripping herself from the others' grips in her sudden change of direction. With both hands, she grabbed the rapier's solid steel guard and yanked. The yelling around her was louder than the ocean's waves.

She took hold of the rapier and swung it point out, sweeping an arc around her. The shouts turned to surprise and panic, and a space cleared around her. Holding the sword level, point out, her grip on the handle steady, she stared at her enemies over the edge of the blade. Now she could handle herself. *Now* she felt a little bit safe and in control.

The men backed away, keeping a good distance around her, as if not sure what to make of her. Some were still chuckling, like this was a game. Several of them had raised their own swords, but made no move toward her. Maybe waiting to see what their bedraggled refugee would do next.

Then things got even stranger.

Across the deck came a shout and the sound of heavy footsteps, hollow on the wood. The men looked suddenly alert—maybe even nervous, and the crowd parted.

The figure who approached, who the rest of the mob

respectfully made way for, wasn't tall and didn't seem powerful like most of the men. She was a woman, sturdy, wearing a long coat belted around her waist, her curly cinnamon hair left loose over her shoulders. She wore a black three-cornered hat and polished boots. Her scowl was hard, angry.

"What have you louts fished up then, eh?" the woman said. When she saw Jill, she frowned, glancing at the bald man from the rowboat. "You found her in the wreckage?"

"Yessir."

Back to Jill now, she said, "What happened, then? How'd you survive the *Newark*'s sinking? Or maybe you were on *Heart's Revenge*?"

Jill couldn't open her mouth to speak, but she shook her head, wondering when she was going to wake up, wondering if she was still underwater, hallucinating or unconscious. So much for feeling safe.

"Speak up, then," said the woman—she must have been the captain here. "Who are you and where'd you come from? Say something, wench, or I'll throw you to these bloody dogs."

At that, the men laughed and growled, like the dogs she'd called them. Jill swept the rapier again, trying to keep that clear space around her. Trying to give herself space to think.

The woman's scowl turned into a half smile and she said, "You think you can use that, then?"

The sword was much heavier than Jill's épée at home. Her arm trembled with the weight of it, and her breaths came in gasps. She didn't know how long she'd be able to fight. But she would fight. She nodded. "Yes."

"Very good. Henry!" the captain called. "You feel like a bit of a game?"

"I do at that, sir." A young man stepped forward, and Jill's heart jumped a little. He was *cute*. Athletic, skin the color of a rich brown wood, short black hair, and a wry smile. Like all the rest, he wore a loose white shirt, loose pants, and went barefoot. And he held a rapier.

He swung the weapon through a few circles like it didn't weigh anything. The crowd, including the captain, pressed back, leaving a wide circle of open deck for them to fight in.

A duel. A freaking duel. She'd lost her last bout—why did she think she had a chance now? She almost dropped the rapier and begged them to have mercy, to not hurt her. But this Henry didn't stop smiling. He even looked like he was laughing at her. That goaded her. The burning, competitive anger that rose up in her was the only familiar thing about the situation.

Henry stood, right foot pointed forward, arm lowered so the rapier's point rested on the deck, and waited for her.

She took a deep breath and steadied herself. Easier said than done when she could feel the floor shifting under her, rocking back and forth unpredictably with the movement of the waves. She reminded herself of her pre-bout mantra: stay calm, keep breathing, don't panic, don't let her opponent fluster her. But she didn't know how she could be more flustered. Which made it all the more important that she keep breathing and stay calm.

She stood *en garde*, right foot forward, left foot back, knees bent. Warily, she saluted him with the rapier she'd stolen and settled her arm into position.

Still seeming amused, Henry saluted her back, flourishing with his off hand and bowing his head besides. Then he stood ready. And why should he be any good, this scruffy-looking kid on a weird sailing ship? No reason she shouldn't be able to take him.

The edge of her rapier gleamed, sharp and dangerous. A real blade, meant for causing harm. For all her bluster, she had never held a sharpened rapier before. She almost stopped the fight right there, but the way the men around her looked at her hadn't changed. They were as dangerous as a real rapier; she had to defend herself. And she would.

He made the first move, reaching out with his blade to tap the end of hers. Nerves and panic made her overreact; she struck his weapon back with a hard beat and jumped back, retreating sloppily. The crowd laughed, and she blushed. That was an amateur move and they all knew it. The captain crossed her arms and frowned.

Before she'd completely settled back into her stance, he struck again, another lazy hit against her blade. But she was ready for it this time and disengaged—dropped her sword slightly so that when he expected to hit it, it wasn't there—and immediately lunged. She caught him off guard that time, and he swung his sword up in a hasty parry and stumbled back. His wide eyes showed surprise. He'd thought he was toying with her. Playing games with a weak opponent. Thought maybe that she was just a girl and no good at this.

Realizing she couldn't rest for a moment in this fight— she had to keep him constantly off guard—she pressed. Lunged again, was blocked again, but moved to attack on a different line.

He crossed to his left, moving in a circle around her, startling her. She shifted to keep up, to keep him in front of her. They were fighting in a circle, not on a strip, like in fencing competition. The change disoriented her. *Just keep him in front of you.*

They exchanged more passes, steel slapping against steel. He drew her thrusts and parried them, that smile still on his face. He was guiding the fight, not her. She tried not to let it make her angry. He never got past her defenses; all her parries were strong, even though her arm burned, and every time their swords met a tingling numbness traveled through her muscles. Her guard fell lower and lower. In a few moments, she wouldn't be able to hold up the sword at all.

When he struck again, she parried like before, but the move brought his blade down and the tip snagged on her pants, just above the knee. The fabric sliced through with a quick ripping sound. Everyone heard it, and Henry jumped back, startled.

She realized then that all of his blows had been at her arms and legs. Because anything else, any stab to her body with a real rapier, would kill her. He wasn't trying to kill her. Her stomach felt sick and roiling at the thought that a slip—any stab that got past her defenses—would really kill her. And she'd been trying to kill him, because she hadn't thought of anything but scoring the touch.

A four-inch slice cut through her pants, a gaping oval exposing skin. No blood; he hadn't broken skin. Suddenly, she couldn't catch her breath. She let her arm drop like a weight, rapier dangling from her hand. Henry looked at her, challenging, gripping his rapier hard like he was ready to go on. He wasn't smiling anymore.

"Knock off there, both of you," the captain called.

They'd already halted the duel, but her order kept them from rushing into another attack—or from expecting an attack from the other. Henry relaxed, lowering his weapon and looking at his captain.

Jill was still trying to slow her breathing, which came in gasps. Her heart was racing. *She would have died, a wrong thrust and she would have died. . . .* And she had been so worried and frustrated about simply losing.

The captain's voice was kind when she spoke to Jill this time. "You know the forms well enough and stand pretty with a sword, but you've never fought for blood, have you, lass?"

Jill could only shake her head—no, she'd never fought for blood. Not real blood. Only ranks, medals, and maybe a college scholarship. She bowed her head, embarrassed, when tears fell. She wiped them away quickly. Her still-wet hair stuck to her cheeks. Salt water crusted her clothing. However much she wanted to sit down, pass out—or drop the rapier, which she wouldn't have been able to raise again even if Henry came at her in another attack—she remained standing before the captain, as straight as she could, which wasn't very at the moment.

"What's your name, lass?"

"Jill. Jill Archer," she said, her voice scratching. She only just noticed that she was thirsty.

"And, Jill, how do you come to be adrift in the wide sea so far from home?"

The tears almost broke then, and she took a moment to answer. "I don't know."

4
FOIBLE

She was Captain Marjory Cooper, and she wasn't the only woman aboard. The handful of other women among the crew dressed like men and blended in. Only the captain wore her hair long and loose and her clothes fitted, showing off her figure. The entire crew, all ages and builds and colors, looked at the captain in awe and didn't hesitate when she sent them back to work. Jill, she ordered to the captain's cabin.

Jill had a random thought: If only Tom and Mandy could see this, the sails and cannons and costumes. Exactly what they'd wanted. They'd be so excited. If only they could be here—and then her gut lurched, because she didn't want her brother and sister anywhere near these people, whoever they were.

Captain Cooper didn't take Jill's stolen rapier from her, and Jill wondered if she really seemed so harmless that she could walk around armed and no one cared. Or if everybody knew that even with a rapier, Jill was alone here and couldn't do anything to hurt them. She had no power. Still, she clung to the weapon like it was a life preserver and felt some small security by having it.

Rapier in hand, Jill wasn't as frightened as she might have been, alone with the captain. But having the rapier didn't mean anything—Jill was too exhausted now to use it. While she was pretty sure she could kick, scratch, and fight if she was in danger—for a little while, at least—beyond that, she was pretty much screwed, just like she thought at first.

The captain had a small room in the back of the ship, below the main deck. At least, it seemed small to Jill, but it must have been the largest quarters aboard. The simple wood-paneled room had a table with a bench in the middle, cupboards on two sides, and a narrow bed in the back. A small glass lantern hung from the central beam, giving only enough light to make out the corners on the furniture. They both had to duck when standing inside, the ceiling was so low.

Captain Cooper offered Jill a tin cup of water. It tasted stale, but it cleared the salt from her mouth and soothed the burning in her throat. Then Cooper kicked the bench, scooting it out from the table, indicating that Jill should sit.

Jill turned gratefully to the seat—her legs were trembling. But the captain stopped her. "Wait. There. What's that in your pocket?"

The outline of the piece of rusted rapier was stark through her wet clothes. Startled, Jill set down the cup and pulled out the broken blade. All she'd been through, and it hadn't fallen out. And still, her hand tingled when she held it. Like it was trying to tell her something, in a voice that sounded like breaking waves.

Captain Cooper held her hand out. Jill wasn't sure she wanted to give her the shard. Then again, Cooper could just take it. Reluctantly, she offered it to Captain Cooper.

Frowning, Cooper held it up to the flickering light, turning it, front and back. With a handkerchief she pulled from the front of her vest, she scrubbed at it for a moment. Rust flaked away in a fine red powder.

The captain's face grew drawn, lips pressing into a tight frown. If Jill didn't think it was impossible, she would have thought the woman sounded nervous. "Tell me true now—were you on the *Newark* when Blane sank it, or were you on the *Heart's Revenge?*"

"Neither," she said. "I was on a tour boat, I fell over by accident—"

"And where did you get this?"

"I found it on the beach. I was just walking and saw it in the sand."

"Found it—just lying there, you say? Then how did you end up in the water? We shouldn't have found anyone, picking through Blane's trash. Blane doesn't give quarter."

"I don't know," she said weakly. "I don't know how I ended up there. I don't know who Blane is."

"Then you don't know where this came from? *Who* it came from?"

"No." Jill pursed her lips and grit her teeth to keep from crying. Tried to stand straight until she realized her legs really were about to give out—they felt like rubber. She sat on the bench. "It probably washed ashore—how could I know where it came from? It's old, hundreds of years old."

"Hundreds of years—" The captain sounded startled. "And where do you come from?"

"The Bahamas. I'm on vacation. We were in a boat, I fell off—"

"You must be addled." The woman was pacing now, just a few steps back and forth across the cabin, and she wouldn't look at Jill.

"I don't know where it came from, and I don't know how I got here," Jill said.

Cooper held up the blade—just a broken scrap of metal. "You're connected to him somehow. Through this."

"How do you even know what it is, how can you recognize it?"

"I'm the one who broke it. It should have been lost forever, and now it's back. Because of you." She pointed the rusted scrap at Jill, who leaned away from it, her heart pounding. Which of them was crazy here?

"But how—"

Cooper shook her head. "No. No more. You aren't making sense. Maybe you will after you've had some rest."

"But my family, the tour boat couldn't have gone too far, I wasn't in the water that long—"

"Lass, there's no other boat around for leagues. You lost your family, and you're lucky to be alive."

"Then take me back to the island, they're probably waiting for me—"

Captain Cooper turned on her. "There's naught but cutthroats and bloody pirates on that island. An't no one's family there, and if yours is then they're fools and'll soon be dead, like as not. You'll stay here, where I can keep an eye on you."

That shut Jill up. It also made her mind stumble. The

Bahamas, an island of pirates? All those stories come to life? Maybe she'd fallen a long ways off her family's tour boat.

So what did she do now?

Captain Cooper kept the piece of rapier. Not that the thing had been much of a good luck charm for Jill. But the captain wouldn't explain why it was important, why it wasn't just a scrap of metal.

She slept in the captain's own bed—"Just for now, don't be getting any pretty ideas"—a mattress in a wooden frame, with rough sheets and a heavy wool blanket. Jill thought she should have slept heavily for hours. But the ship's movements kept her awake. Slow, arrhythmic swaying, rocking her one way and another on the hard mattress that might have been stuffed with straw. She started to feel nauseated and wasn't sure it was all from the boat's rocking. Shutting her eyes tight, she tried not to think of it.

Jill slept lightly and with dreams of falling, of being underwater and not being able to swim. She was a good swimmer; nothing should have been able to keep her from the surface. But something was holding her down, anchoring her. And she thrashed awake; the dreaming sense of vertigo didn't go away. She was still on a ship surrounded by strangers, uncertain of the place and time. She'd never felt so helpless.

Well, she'd wanted to get away from everyone, hadn't she?

The motion of the ship had increased, rolling so much that the lantern hanging from the roof beam swung back and forth, and she would have slammed against the bed's frame if she hadn't braced herself. Nothing was loose in the cabin—everything was shut up in cupboards, and the table and floor were clear. Anything loose would be falling all around her. The ship seemed to be riding over hills, making animal-like groans around her.

She was going to throw up. Her stomach seemed to be lurching in the opposite direction from the ship, and though she covered her mouth with her hands, she couldn't stop it. Bile surged up.

A bucket—solid wood, heavy and stable—stood against the wall. As if it had been set there in expectation. She stumbled out of bed and bent over it without looking inside, just in time. She heaved over and over, losing everything she'd eaten that day, and then some. She wouldn't have thought her stomach could hold so much.

Then the acrid stench of it hit her and made her heave again.

Finally, she turned away, sitting heavily, her back to the wall, catching her breath. She wiped her mouth on the tail of her shirt because it was all she had. Her cup of water was gone—of course, it would have emptied all over the cabin by now. Dizzy, her choices were to keel over, go to sleep and never wake up again, or go outside and get some fresh air. Assuming she could look ahead without her vision swaying in front of her.

Using the frame of the bed, she pulled herself to her feet. Her first step made her stumble—the floor wasn't where it should have been. To go the straight line from the bed to the door, she made a zigzagging path across the floor, following the ship's rocking. But she reached the door and leaned there, shutting her eyes and catching her breath, determined not to be sick again. Doggedly, she gripped the latch on the door and opened it.

Captain Marjory Cooper, her smile crooked and her gaze hard, stood blocking her way. "I heard you were up. Feeling better then?"

Jill swallowed, hoping to keep her stomach steady. But she didn't dare open her mouth, just in case. The captain pushed her back into the cabin.

"You've not spent much time at sea, have you?"

Jill shook her head and tried to guess if Cooper's smile was meant to be comforting or mocking.

She had in hand a few pieces of clothing: a loose, long-sleeved shirt, cotton pants, and a soft cap. The clothing Jill arrived in wasn't so out of place here—her clamdiggers were like the trousers that many of the sailors on board wore, and her tank top was just a shirt. But the captain handed her the new items.

"You'll burn like a lobster in the sun in those things. You need to cover up until you get a good tan on you. It'll keep the men from looking too hard at you as well. These should fit you. They're cabin-boy sized."

Reluctantly, Jill took the clothing. Changing clothes made her situation—lost at sea on a boat full of strangers—seem permanent. She felt like a prisoner. She ought to get out of here—and go where? "What's going to happen to me?"

"We'll have to discuss that, won't we? When you're dressed, come up on deck."

Jill was actually happy to get out of the scratchy, salt-laden clothes she'd nearly drowned in. But she thought she looked like a bum in the loose clothes. No—she looked like a pirate. She kept her bra on—it made her feel a little more like herself. Like it could shield her. She also brought out the rapier, which she'd kept with her on the bunk. Since no one said anything, she was going to carry the weapon.

When she opened the door and came out on the deck, she hesitated, amazed.

All the sails were unfurled, and the wind filled them. Above her, a collage of rippling white canvas rose up on tall masts. Bright sun gleamed on them, almost blinding. Beyond

them, the sky was blue, and white specks—seagulls—
danced and wheeled in the wind above the ship. Around
her was ocean, wide and blue, and the ship skimmed across
waves, sleek as a fish. She reached up and felt wind brushing
her fingers, ruffling her hair. For a moment, she felt like she
could step into the air and float.

"You! Lass! Over here!" The captain called to her from
the back of the ship, on the other side of the hatch and stairs
leading below. There was an honest-to-God wheel here, half
her height, with handles protruding off the spokes. Just
like in the movies. This was all like a movie. She had to be
dreaming.

Cooper had tied a piece of string around the middle of
the rapier shard so that it dangled, balanced and horizontal.
She held the end of the string at arm's length and watched,
along with the two men with her—the bald man from the
rowboat and another, dark-skinned, his hair in long braids
tied back with a bandanna. He gave Jill a smile, and she
looked away.

Though the ship rocked and shifted, the rapier tip
remained pointing in one direction.

That wasn't possible, the way it remained motionless,
frozen in place despite dangling in midair. It was just a piece
of metal. . . . Jill stared at it. She wanted to touch it, feel the
surface again, just to be sure. But she'd have had to reach

past Captain Cooper to do it, so she didn't.

The shard had been cleaned and oiled—very little of the rust remained, though the steel was still rough and corroded, with a reddish sheen of tarnished metal. But a pattern was visible now, curling lines like waves engraved on the flat of the blade.

"It'll be our compass," the captain explained, at Jill's wondering expression. "It wants to return to its master. And however far it's traveled, you've brought it right back, girl, haven't you?"

"I don't know how I got here," Jill said. She kept telling her, and Cooper kept not believing her. "How is it doing that?"

Cooper gave her an odd, considering look. Then shook her head. "Blane's looking for it, too, I reckon. I'm lucky I got to you first. Hell, *you're* lucky I got to you first. Assuming you're not spying for him."

"I don't know what you're talking about at all—who is Blane?" Jill's hand clenched on the handle of her borrowed rapier. Not that she could do anything with it; that guy Henry proved that. The wire wrapping on the grip pressed into her palm; she wanted to hit something with it, no matter how little good it would do.

"Settle down, there. Know what I think? However you got here, whatever it means, you'll lead me to him. Then I'll have done with him for good. Now, what to do with you in the meantime?"

Just let me go, Jill thought, but to say it would have sounded whiny, weak. She had a feeling these people wouldn't think much of her at all, if they thought her weak. So she kept silent and glared.

The captain put a hand on her hip. "You look like you've had a lot of soft living, but anyone on the *Diana* who expects to eat gets put to work."

"I don't know anything about sailing," Jill argued.

"You don't have to, to scrub the deck."

Why would anyone bother scrubbing the deck of a sailing ship that was constantly getting wet, salty, and stepped on? You'd have to scrub it every day.

"Captain," the black man said, his smile sly. "She should sign the articles if she's going to be on the crew."

"I don't know if she is, Abe," said Cooper, answering his grin. Jill blinked at them both, confused. "Jenks, fetch the book."

"Aye, sir," said the bald man in a sandpaper voice, and he ran from the deck to the cabin below.

"Can you read, girl?" the captain said.

"Of course I can."

The laugh in Captain Cooper's eyes grew brighter at that, and Jill bristled at the thought they were making fun of her. This was all a bad joke.

"The articles keep the law aboard a ship like ours. Read 'em through." Jenks arrived with the book, which Cooper opened and handed to Jill.

The book was a slim, tall thing; she needed two hands to hold it and had to tuck the rapier under her arm. It was bound in leather and water stained. The articles only took up one page; the rest of the pages were filled with signatures. Her eyes needed a moment to focus on the dense writing, black ink on a yellowed page. The handwriting was crooked, cramped, and hard to read. *S*'s looked like *f*'s and whole words were abbreviated, and the author seemed to assume she'd know what it all meant. But she'd said she could read and refused to ask for help. The others didn't comment on how long it took her.

The articles stated that the crew elected the captain and quartermaster and could remove them at any time by an organized vote, which seemed awfully orderly and civilized. There were punishments—flogging—for crimes: Theft, murder, and rape were specifically noted. The articles also laid out the compensation a crew member would get for injuries sustained in battle—different amounts of gold for hands lost, legs lost, and blindness—and described how prizes were to be split—everyone got an equal share, even the captain.

"You're pirates," Jill said, reading the page again, approaching full-on panic. She had to get out of here.

The captain laughed. "Pirates! We're enterprising business folk!" The men around her chuckled at the joke, and Jill blushed. "Lass," the captain continued. "If you're not on the crew, then you're a prisoner and you'll stay locked up below."

This was crazy. Could she tell them just to drop her back off at Nassau? But their Nassau wasn't her Nassau. Nothing but water surrounded them. Where could she go?

What were the chances that any of this would apply to her? She could be careful and follow the rules, avoid offending anyone—though according to the articles fighting among crew was prohibited and she'd already broken that one in her duel with Henry. But she hadn't been crew then. And she wouldn't fight in any battles and be in danger of losing limbs. Surely she'd get home before that happened. Somehow she'd wake up from whatever dream this was.

If she were on deck—not locked up—she had a chance of escaping. They had to stop at land sometime. Then she'd run. Then she—she didn't know, but she'd figure it out.

The captain turned to the next page in the book, revealing rows with a few names, but more *X*'s. Most of the people who'd signed couldn't read. Jenks had also brought a pen—no, a feather, a long quill with most of the feathers shaved off—and a little bottle of ink. He held the ink while Marjory dipped the pen in it, then handed it to Jill.

"So what'll it be? Crew or no?"

Jill didn't know what other choice she had. She took the pen and signed her name on the next open space. Her writing looked large, round, and clumsy next to the other signatures. The others leered like they'd won a victory.

Surely it didn't mean anything, she thought.

Cooper blew on the ink to dry it and handed book and quill back to Jenks.

"Welcome aboard, Jill. You've met me. Your quartermaster is Abe"—she nodded at the smiling black man—"and first mate is Jenks." The bald man snarled. "Now you'll scrub the deck."

Jill stared. She didn't even know what scrubbing decks meant. Scrubbing with a mop? A brush?

"And give me that sword, won't you? And you'll say, 'Aye, sir' when I give you an order."

If this was a joke, she was the only one not laughing. They were teasing her, and she couldn't do anything about it. Anger made her straighten and look Captain Cooper in the eye. The woman might not have been so tall; she didn't even look strong. But Jill wouldn't want to fight her. Cooper wouldn't fight fair. In the captain's mind—and in the minds of the crew—by signing that page she'd agreed to obey the captain, no arguments. She wondered if pirates really did make people walk the plank. This time, there might not be anyone to fish her out.

"Aye, sir," she said softly, offering the rapier, handle first, to Cooper. The woman's smile was thin, satisfied.

Cooper turned over the wheel and shouted, "Henry! Show the new recruit how we scrub decks!"

"Aye!" He'd been coiling rope with another sailor by the side of the ship, but he looked gleeful when Cooper called to him.

Henry, the boy she'd fought. Who might have beaten her if the captain hadn't stopped the duel. She didn't want to face him. Cooper pulled him aside, and Jill caught a few whispered words: "Make sure Jenks and his crowd keep away from her."

"Aye," he murmured back. Jill pretended not to hear, but she worried.

Cooper straightened and called, "Off you go. Welcome to the *Diana*."

Jill didn't feel very welcome. She'd play along just until she could find a way to get out of here. Somehow. But it was hard to escape from a boat in the middle of the ocean. Land was still in sight—a rough band of foliage on the horizon. But she didn't know if it was the Bahamas, and she didn't think she could swim so far.

Then Henry was standing before her holding a brick-size rock, like a pumice stone, and a bucket. "Don't take it personal. The newest bloke always scrubs the decks." He held the stone and bucket out to her.

The deck, which was probably only sixty feet long and twenty feet wide, suddenly looked as large as a football field. "The whole thing?" she said. "With this?"

"Now you can guess why it's always the job of the new bloke." He was enjoying this.

"But . . . I mean why bother? People walk around on this all day. It'll never stay clean. Why bother scrubbing it?"

"You don't know? Really?" She looked blankly at him. "It's the damp, the salt air, the mildew. It'll rot the wood if we don't keep it scrubbed. Wait'll we have to careen her and scrub the rot off the hull. There's a bloody dire job."

Stone in hand, Jill knelt and dreaded starting because it would take forever. She started in one corner in the back and ran the stone over the wood, polishing it. The deck was pale and smooth from all the previous scrubbing.

Henry watched, sitting up on the side, leaning against a length of rigging, whittling on a piece of wood with a penknife, dropping shavings on her nice clean deck. Teasing her.

"Do you have to sit there?" she said.

"I need to keep a close eye on you. Make sure you don't

miss an inch. Try scrubbing in circles, it works better."

So she did, shifting sideways, until she'd reached the other side of the ship. Then she worked her way back. She could feel Henry watching her, an itching down her spine. He seemed to be far too pleased, watching her working on her hands and knees. Like he was gloating.

"I gotta ask," he said, putting the knife away. "Where'd you learn to fight so pretty? Like a picture in a book, you are. That's no use in a real fight."

A real fight—that tournament *was* real fighting. At least, she'd thought so then. It was all this that wasn't real. She paused a moment to glare at him. Just like she thought, he was teasing, and he didn't let up. "I'm just trying to figure out what your story is. Most of us have pretty good stories, but you, finding you alive in that wreckage—seems like it ought to be right impressive."

"I don't know what happened," she said, her voice flat.

"Don't be sore. I'm just trying to be friendly," he said.

She glared again. She wasn't in the mood.

"Don't you want to know how I ended up here?"

"Not really."

"I was a lad on a merchant ship that the *Diana* captured. I got much the same offer you did, sign on with the crew here or be set adrift. But I didn't have to think it over. My old captain was a mean one. A right bastard. Held back rations to raise profits, and us at the low end got shillings for our troubles, never mind shares. I tell you true, this place is a world better than where I came from. I wouldn't trade it."

In spite of herself, she'd stopped scrubbing to listen to him, trying to imagine the world he might have come from. And she couldn't. "I don't belong here at all," she said.

"Then you're not one of those girls dresses up as a lad and goes looking for adventure?"

"No. I keep telling you, it was an accident."

"You look it, with your hair cut. It's what we all thought."

"I—I'm not sure what happened."

"Lost your memory, then?"

"Yeah, I guess I did," she murmured. It seemed as good an explanation as any.

By the end of the day, the ship had lost sight of land. No chance of swimming for it now.

She must have worked ten straight hours that day. Henry was called away on another chore, something to do with the sails, but Jill couldn't stop working because someone was always around, climbing rigging, mending sails, keeping lookout, or doing one of the other mysterious jobs on a boat like this. She scrubbed, and her hands and arms grew cramped, her fingers sore and cracked, and the sun beat down on her. She'd never worked so hard and could feel herself getting sunburned, despite the long sleeves and pants. Her nose, ears, and the back of her neck stung.

As they sailed on, the view never changed, and she had no indication that time was passing except for the sun moving overhead.

It was almost at the horizon when Henry returned and took the stone from her, grabbing it right out of her hands. She stared at her empty hands a moment, then looked at him, almost hurt. She wasn't done yet—at least she didn't think she was. But she might have gone around the whole deck twice for all she knew.

"Come on then, time for supper," he said, and gestured her toward the middle of the deck.

She needed a long moment to stand, straightening the kinks out of her back. She'd thought she was in good shape.

The crew, thirty or forty people, gathered in the widest, most open part of the ship and made a rowdy line in front of two men, who carried what looked like a cast iron pot and a small wooden barrel: dinner.

Jill was starving, but she hung back, not wanting to get caught in a brawl. She couldn't tell if the yelling and jostling was in earnest or in fun. But no fighting broke out among them—just like the articles said.

Abe stood near the men with the food, facing out, supervising. Abe was the quartermaster and almost as important as the captain on a ship like this. He was in charge of supplies, rations, and treasure, and of ensuring that everyone got an equal share and that no one tried to take more behind the others' backs. This position was, like the captain's, elected, and the quartermaster was the one everyone trusted. When he saw Jill, he smiled, but like with Henry she couldn't tell if he was laughing at her or honestly trying to be friendly. After all his talk, Henry hadn't seemed to hold the grudge against her. She looked at every member of the crew, searching for the hostility they'd shown when she first came on board. Mostly, they ignored her.

At sunset, lanterns were hung about the deck, from hooks on the masts and railings, and the cook—a thin, bearded man who didn't look anywhere near clean enough to be serving food—distributed supper under Abe's watchful gaze. Henry found Jill a tin cup and a dented metal bowl. She waited at the end of the line because she didn't want anyone staring over her shoulder. And no one could give her a hard time if she put herself at the end. She wanted to hide, mouselike. But she also wanted to eat.

Then she got a look at what the cook was serving, smelled it—and it didn't smell like food. Overcooked, vaguely rotten, vaguely stale. She wasn't hungry anymore.

When she reached the cook, Abe handed her a plate, already filled with a spoonful of cooked potatoes, dried meat, and a roll that was so hard it rattled. "Take that to the prisoner, belowdecks and aft."

She frowned. "Another job for the rookie?" she said. Abe only shrugged.

She went to the hatch and down the steps below. Steps—it was almost a ladder, they were so steep and narrow. As she eased herself down, she kept a grip on the side.

While she still didn't know her way around the ship, she figured it couldn't be that hard to find someone. The ship wasn't that large. But she suddenly couldn't remember which way was aft. After looking back and forth for a moment, into the creaking shadows, she gave up and called out, "Is there a prisoner down here?" She walked along the center of the hold, calling, feeling ridiculous.

"Here." A muffled voice came from farther back. Jill quickened her pace, moving among hammocks, crates, bundles of ropes, and barrels of who knew what.

In the very rear of the ship was a small room, no bigger than a closet, with an iron latch on the outside. This must be it. She slid the latch back and opened the wooden door.

Some lantern light came through a row of holes in the roof that must have led up to the deck; Jill could make out a few details. A man was sitting on a plain bench. He wore a grungy shirt that might have been white once, open at the collar; tan-colored trousers; and worn boots. His sandy hair was tied in a short ponytail. He was older, middle aged maybe, with a cynical glare in his eyes. He leaned back against the wall and regarded her.

"New recruit?" he asked, a wry quirk to his lips.

She stared fishlike for a moment before handing him the plate. "Here."

"Ah. I'm overjoyed," he said flatly, but he took the platter and dug in, scooping the potatoes with his fingers.

"So what do you have to do to get locked up on a pirate ship?" she asked.

"I didn't sign the articles. Not like you did, I wager."

She felt herself blush; but she was also relieved that she had signed and wasn't locked up here with him.

"If I may make an observation, you don't seem much like the pirating type. What was it, you thought you didn't have a choice?" he said. "So where'd they find you? They're so desperate now they're taking girls? You should be in a kitchen somewhere, wearing a skirt and apron and baking bread. Instead you've found yourself among true heathens."

He was right, she didn't belong here. But he wasn't any more likely to understand what had happened to her, so she kept her mouth shut.

He leaned forward, dropping his voice to a whisper; she

tried not to flinch away. "Here's some advice—keep your wits about you. This ship won't sail free forever. When you decide you don't want to hang with the rest of the dogs, I can help you."

"Why would you help me?"

"Well—it might be that we can help each other, when the time is right. Think on it, why don't you."

She slipped out of the cell, shut and locked the door. She didn't know what to make of the guy—and she could already tell him she didn't want to hang with anybody.

She was adrift on an alien world. The clothes they wore, the ship, the work, the smells, the words they used—all of it was wrong, and she was exhausted from trying to figure it out.

Back on deck, the cook had a plate of food waiting for her—and the food didn't even smell right. She'd have to eat, sooner or later—and what kind of dream would make her eat food like this? Next, she watched the cook fill a tin cup from a tap in a small barrel.

He gave it to her, and she raised it to her face to see what it was. The liquid had an amber tinge to it, and it stung her eyes and made her wrinkle her nose. Not water, then.

"What is it?" she asked Abe.

"What is it?" echoed Henry, who was nearby, laughing, unbelieving. "It's got rum in it."

Oh, her mother would be horrified at this. Well, she'd wanted to try it. Carefully, Jill brought the mug to her lips.

This didn't smell sugary and fruity like those endless rounds of rum punch or her mother's pretty drinks with slices of pineapple in them. This was acrid and seemed more like rubbing alcohol than something you'd drink. She took a bare sip; fumes filled her sinuses and the liquid burned her tongue. Surprised, she drew back, blinking away tears.

The pirates laughed. One of the women, hair in a braid and scarf on her head, yelled, "That's no way to take yer grog, you tadpole! Bottoms up!" The woman tipped back her own mug to demonstrate.

Bottoms up. If they could do it, so could she. She tipped back her head and poured the rum into her mouth, figuring if she drank it fast enough, she wouldn't taste anything.

Her whole mouth—lips, tongue, throat, everything—turned to fire, puckered, went tingling, then numb. She started coughing, which made them all laugh harder, but she was too busy gasping for breath to notice. Then she felt warm. It started as a heat in her stomach, which spread out to her limbs like syrup, thick and sticky. Then she felt very, very relaxed. She might have taken her brain out of her head and put it on a shelf. And that was okay. It meant she didn't flinch back in a panic like she might have done when Henry put a hand on her arm.

"Think maybe you'd better sit down, eh?" he said.

"I'm fine, I'm fine," she murmured, but she let Henry guide her to a convenient barrel, where she reached behind her because the seat seemed to be moving. Or she was.

"Cor, I reckon the tadpole ain't never had a drink before," one of them said. More laughter. Jill still had her plate of food, and she was still starving.

The pirates were settled into impromptu seats around the deck, perched on the side or on barrels or on the deck itself. Noisy and eager, they ate with their fingers, and since she didn't have a choice, so did she. The food didn't taste too bad—but the rum may have killed her taste buds. Maybe that was the point.

As they drained their rum, the crew grew louder, laughing harder, trading jokes and insults, punching each other until one of them fell over, which made them all laugh even more. Then one of them pulled out a fiddle, and another had a silver pipe, just a little longer than the length of his hand. They began to play.

It was like folk music, bright like birds singing, and soon people began to clap, stomp their feet, and sing along, but so loud and slurred that Jill couldn't make out words. Her rum was almost gone, and the light from the lanterns had turned to halos in her wavering sight.

This was like a story. Golden lantern light played on

wood, rope, and canvas; the ship became a bubble of light and music traveling through a shadowed world. She'd fallen out of her world and into this one, where the words and voices were strange. The stars were huge and bright, and a three-quarters moon rose, turning the sea to silver.

Later, many of the pirates seemed to fall over and sleep where they were rather than make their way to proper beds. She didn't even know if the boat had proper beds apart from the captain's, but the way her head was spinning she thought maybe she ought to find out. She could sleep and figure out what to do in the morning. Maybe they'd be at a port, and she could find a phone to call her parents.

Even though she was pretty sure she wouldn't find any phones.

Jill blinked to focus and say something about beds, but the deck was moving at the edges of her vision. Because it was a boat. And the waves rolled, and her stomach flopped. She bent over and lost everything she'd eaten and drunk, right on the deck she'd spent so much time scrubbing clean. She could feel the start of a pounding headache.

"God help you, you are a tadpole."

People were there, one on each arm, and they pulled her up, and the world flopped again, but her stomach went with it this time and didn't empty itself.

"I can walk, I'm fine," she tried to say, but the words came out wrong because her tongue wouldn't work right. So that was rum. Why had she wanted so badly to try it, again? It turned out she couldn't walk very well after all, because they brought her to stairs she couldn't even see. By then her eyes were closed.

She heard the captain say, "Any of you vermin takes advantage of the girl in this state I'll have his hide. Understood?"

"Aye."

Still laughing, but softly, they put her in a bed that rocked her to sleep like she was a baby in a cradle. Or it might have been that she just passed out.

5

FLÈCHE

Jill woke up cramped, uncomfortable, with a headache that grew worse, throbbing at her temples, when she tried to sit up, which she couldn't do very well because she was rolled into a hammock. The ship was still rocking, and the hammock, suspended from the beam above, swung with the motion. Like the rest of the ship, the room she was in smelled of damp wood, salt, and slime, and it was dark. The only light came in through the hatch at one end. Bright sunlight. Even though she was twenty feet away from it, she squinted and turned away. Some dream this was. She ought to be able to skip over this part.

Her head hurt every time she moved.

She was below the main deck. Hammocks hung from every beam, maybe two dozen of them, in a space that didn't seem very large. Most of those were empty, swaying with the creaking ship. The few bodies that lay sleeping here didn't seem much better off than she was; they were either snoring in deep sleep or groaning in hungover pain.

"There you are, awake at last!" Henry climbed down the steep stairs and blocked the sunlight from the hatch. Jill wondered how she'd made it down those narrow steps last night.

A couple of the others moaned louder and grumbled insults at Henry, who grinned at them.

Henry came over to her and loomed. She rolled out of the hammock just to keep him from staring down at her. Her balance still wasn't working right, though; she landed on her knees and had to hold on to the hammock's ropes to keep from falling further. She glared at him.

"Bright eyed and ready to start the day, I see."

"I want to go home. This is a mistake." Slowly, moving her head as little as possible, she pulled herself to her feet.

"Nonsense. You signed on, you're crew now. Time to get to work."

She wondered if this was punishment—she'd wanted to get away from her life, and here she'd gotten her wish.

Maybe she should just go along for the ride, until she woke up for real.

She wasn't sure she could let go of the hammock yet. She didn't seem to be able to stand up straight and kept swaying with the motion of the boat. "What if I say no?"

Henry shrugged. "Then you don't eat. Or maybe we'll pitch you over the side."

Someone laughed. Someone always seemed to be laughing, mocking.

She followed Henry to the steps and up to the deck.

"Is there any water?" she said, thinking a gallon of water would make her feel a tiny bit better.

There was, stored in a barrel on deck at the front of the ship. Henry had recovered her tin cup, which still smelled of rum and sent Jill's head spinning again. But she drank two cupfuls of water and felt much better.

For another day, she scrubbed decks.

She forgot about being seasick, and forgot about being scared of the pirates. Mostly, it was strange, because they didn't act like terrifying criminals or happy-go-lucky cartoon pirates. They worked—the chores on board seemed never ending: cleaning, repairing, working on the sails and rigging, working on weapons, sharpening knives and checking pistols. Amidst all that they seemed laid-back, easygoing, enjoying drinking and singing, and they seemed to respect the captain, who stayed on deck most of the day, watching the crew or the sea. Jill supposed that they all had to get along well, or they wouldn't survive very long cooped up on the tiny ship for weeks at a time.

She kept expecting to wake up from a dream. Being here, among the constant ripple of sails, the forest of mast and rigging, seeing nothing but ocean around them, was so surreal, it couldn't be happening. When she fell overboard, maybe she'd been knocked on her head and was lying on a hospital bed in a coma. That seemed more likely. But she could smell salt on the air, and she tasted the sea on her lips.

She wondered if her parents were looking for her. Or sitting next to her hospital bed, holding her hand, begging her to wake up. Jill thought she should have known what was happening, if that was the case. She ought to hear her mother yelling at Mandy and Tom in the background.

A third day passed, then a fourth. Jill's skin dried out and browned, and she could now walk across the deck in a straight line no matter how much the ship swayed.

Henry stopped supervising her on every little chore, but they continued talking. He showed her the ropes, literally, teaching her how the rigging worked, how the sails worked, what they all needed to do when the commands were given, working as a team to keep the ship moving. He seemed to be the youngest one on board, close to her own age even, though it was hard to judge ages here. They all might have been young, but worn out from hard work and living in the elements. Like that grizzled, wiry tour guide.

Jill had the impression that the captain was always watching her—like she still thought Jill was a spy for this Blane guy, and that she'd give herself away eventually. Marjory Cooper was intimidating; Jill felt herself grow smaller under the woman's gaze. But Cooper was better than some of the others who seemed to study her when they thought no one was looking. Jenks, the bald first mate, for one.

According to the articles the pirates had a law against rape—the punishment was being marooned, set alone on a beach with a bottle of water and a pistol with one shot loaded. Jill would rather not find out how well the ship enforced its own rules, and stuck close to Henry, Abe, some of the crew who'd been friendly to her, and even the captain.

Jill was scrubbing the deck near the wheel—the helm, Henry called it—when Abe called the captain over and handed her a telescope—no, a spyglass. A brass cylinder on a lanyard. The captain brought the instrument to her own eye.

Looking out to what they studied, Jill couldn't see anything. She squinted into the bright sunlight reflecting off the water, all the way to the haze on the horizon, and saw only ocean. But Cooper and Abe saw something.

"On its way to the market at Havana, I'll wager. It's off our course," Captain Cooper said finally, handing the telescope back. She took the broken piece of rapier from her pocket and suspended it on its string. The length of steel swung for just a moment before pointing solidly in one direction—leaning, almost, in defiance of gravity. West, Jill thought, while the object of their attention was southeast.

It was just a chunk of rusted metal. No magic to it at all. But then, how had she come here? No, it was all a dream, she reminded herself. It didn't have to make sense.

"But, Captain," Abe said, wearing his constant wry smile. "We must, yes?"

The captain set her jaw and sighed. "I suppose we must." She turned away from the rail and hollered, bellowing so that her voice carried over the whole ship, to the top of the masts.

"Ready about! Hoist the colors, ye dogs!"

A cheer went up, adding to the noise, until it sounded like a storm, thunder and rain pounding against wood. Then sailors ran to their duties.

Jenks was at the helm and spun the wheel. The *Diana* heaved over, tipping as it changed direction. Jill stumbled a couple of steps but didn't fall, braced, and considered it a victory.

The vessel, which had been traveling peacefully, cutting through waves on what seemed to be a gentle breeze, became fierce. It slammed into the next set of waves, and water sprayed up, over the railing. Sails slacked and rippled, seemingly confused for a moment, before finding the wind again and filling, wide and taut, sounding like cracks of thunder. The ship raced forward. Hoisted on a line, a black flag rose to the top of the mainmast. It showed an image in white: a leering skull, with a sword and stemmed rose crossed beneath it. Captain Cooper's flag.

Shouting and calling, members of the crew rushed over the deck. It looked chaotic to Jill. No one seemed to have any direction in mind, but the purpose soon began to emerge: several men came from belowdecks carrying armloads of weapons—swords and guns. Others grabbed the weapons and distributed them, until everyone was armed.

Henry passed by with a sword in hand, and Jill held his arm to stop him. "What am I supposed to do?"

He looked at her, looked out to sea, then at the captain. He seemed to be debating whether to annoy Captain Cooper with such a problem. The answer must have been no, because he said, "Well, we've seen you're not a fighter, so you'd best get below."

But she could fight, she *was* a fighter, they'd seen her handle a sword and hold her own against Henry. But the captain had been right, and she'd never fought for blood, and she didn't want to have to kill anyone. So better that she stay out of the way.

Ahead now, Jill could see it—another ship, so far away it looked like a toy, bobbing on the waves. The *Diana* raced toward it. Jill couldn't tell which way the wind was blowing—the sails above her seemed to be moving in a storm of breeze, sound, and motion. But the direction didn't matter, because they were definitely drawing closer to the other ship. It was much larger than the *Diana*, with three masts and a crowd of sails. But it was slower. While the *Diana* skimmed over the waves, moving fast and sending up sprays of white, the other ship swayed along at the mercy of the waves.

Jill couldn't quite bring herself to go belowdecks.

The crew gathered, preparing to attack, and it wasn't what Jill was expecting. They didn't look like warriors ready for battle—trained, lined up, weapons prepared. Instead, they stood on the side of the ship, or clung to parts of the rigging, baring their teeth and shouting curses. Some of them fired their guns, making noise and putting black puffs of smoke in the air, which began to smell like burned sulfur. A pair of the cannons had been rolled forward, and doors in the side of the ship opened so the mouths protruded, visible to the other ship. A couple of men held lit torches, waving them over their heads, which seemed like a terrible thing to do on a wooden boat. Others shook their swords, held daggers in their teeth, jumped from mast to deck and back again, and screamed with laughter. A few had smeared lines of soot on their cheeks; a few others had taken off their hats and shaken out their hair to make it wild and tangled.

They looked like madmen.

As they drew close to the other ship, Jill could see the other crew running in a panic. Men on the masts began loosening lines, letting sails hang heavy and useless, leaving their ship effectively helpless, dead in the water. A flag that had been flying on the central mast—it had a red and white pattern, but Jill couldn't identify it—disappeared.

A man in a fancy, decorated coat stood by the side closest to the *Diana* and waved a white handkerchief over his head.

The other ship was surrendering without a fight.

The crew of the *Diana* cheered and fired another round from their pistols. Captain Cooper, who'd been watching the other ship through her spyglass, Abe at her side, lowered the instrument and gave a nod of satisfaction.

"Jenks, prepare for boarding. Let's put on a good show for them," she said. The first mate shouted orders. Ropes and hooks appeared, the helm turned, and the sails went slack as the ship slowed and came up alongside the other.

It was all a show. Side by side, the *Diana* was clearly smaller than the other ship, which was wide, large, and presumably packed with cargo. But it didn't seem to have any cannons or as many crew members—only a dozen stood on the deck. Maybe it could have outrun them, but it hadn't even tried. The *Diana's* crew had won by intimidation. Somehow, it made them even more frightening than if they had won by force.

The crew who were involved with throwing ropes and hooks over to the other ship continued hanging on the side, brandishing weapons, shouting war cries and insults to the other crew, who watched, backing away from the side, wide-eyed and cowering.

The *Diana's* crew put woven mats over the side to buffer and protect the hulls and used the ropes to pull the other ship close and secure it. A group of the pirates—still armed, still wild and cackling—escorted their captain over the side and to the other ship. Abe, Jenks, and Henry were among them. Jill moved closer to the side to watch.

The other crew stumbled and scurried away from the approaching pirates. The other captain, the man in the fancy coat—bright green material, with gold braid and buttons—approached, though warily. When Captain Cooper emerged to greet him, the other captain quailed.

"Oh God, it's you!"

"That's right, sir, you have been captured by that bloody pirate queen, harridan of the waves and witch of the sea. And you are very, very wise to offer yourselves so freely. Though

I rather wish you'd put up a fight—I'm disappointed I won't be murdering you and sinking your boat. Now—one word of argument from any of you and I will." She made a stunning picture standing before him, hands on hips, her coat buttoned, her high boots polished, her hat firm on her long, curling hair, and her face like that of an avenging goddess. Her mob of demons was arrayed around her.

The other captain was on his knees now. "Please, have mercy, I have a wife at home, small children—a daughter! Be merciful, they'll be lost without me!"

"On the contrary I rather suspect they'd be better off, given what you are."

"What—" the captain stammered, then went silent.

Jill straightened, curious, as if the movie in front of her had just gotten to the good part.

"Abe. Bring 'em up," Marjory said, never looking away from her captured counterpart.

The quartermaster called to several of the crewmates, who followed him down the dark hatch into the ship's hold.

Just as they'd captured them, the *Diana*'s crew held back their victims by intimidation and possibly reputation. Their seeming madness inspired fear. The other crew cowered, shoving at each other to get farther away from the pirates, and never made a move to resist.

Jill expected Abe and the others to carry up crates, boxes, barrels. Maybe even sacks of gold. The treasure from a million pirate stories. But that's not what emerged from below.

Abe guided a person, holding the man's arm, helping him step carefully. He was thin, weak, barely able to stand. He moved slowly, shuffling—iron bands and chains weighed down his ankles. His skin was black, his dark hair short and matted. Abe led the man onto the deck and to the side. Behind him came another man with chains banded to his ankles. Behind him, another. And another, and another. Abe and the others led twenty men and women in chains onto the deck.

This was a slave ship.

"Valuable cargo, isn't it then?" Marjory said to the slaver captain.

"I just transport 'em. That's all, where's the fault?"

Captain Cooper planted her foot on his shoulder and shoved. He sprawled and begged again for mercy.

When the slaves were all on deck, Abe began leading them over the side to the *Diana*. It took a long time. With the iron chains, they moved so slowly. Many looked sick besides, thin and weak. They all had red sores where the bands cut into their skin. As they came aboard, they passed by Jill where she leaned on the side. They never looked up; their heads were bowed, their eyes downcast. She wanted to reach out to them, offer some kind of comfort, but she didn't know what to say. So she just watched.

Now that some of the gun smoke had cleared, a new smell tinged the air, drifting from the other ship. The smell of illness, of people living packed together without washing, without clean water, without anything. This had stopped being anything like a movie. Or a dream. This couldn't be a dream. Jill didn't have the imagination to produce a dream—nightmare—like this. This wasn't a dream, and she wasn't going to wake up.

Back on the slave ship, Captain Cooper was looming over her prisoner.

"I think I will also be taking that pretty coat from you."

When he didn't move quickly enough, she grabbed the collar and pulled as he tried to scuttle away. With little apparent effort, Cooper twisted and yanked, and the coat was off and in her hands. She tossed it to Henry, turned away from her prisoner, and never looked back.

To her own crew she said, "Move on, scurvy dogs, scour this wreck for what we can use. Quick now, so's not to spend more time among scum than we need to."

This was obviously a process they'd been through before. Several of the crew kept watch over the prisoners on the deck of the captured ship, keeping muskets trained on them and threatening death. The rest went all over the ship, looking in crates, trunks, and casks. The sounds of smashing and breaking carried from belowdecks; the slaver captain winced at every jolt.

Soon, a procession started from the other ship to the *Diana*, crew members carrying not just wooden boxes and crates, but also coils of rope, bundles of sailcloth, and other tools and equipment of obvious use on a sailing ship. None of it was the kind of treasure Tom had gone on about. But Jill considered—what good would chests of gold do out here? These supplies would keep the *Diana* sailing for months.

"Move aside, Tadpole, if you can't be of any use," Jenks grumbled at her when he came over the side, too close to where Jill was lurking. She scrambled away, but glared after him. He'd gone out of his way to bother her.

The whole operation took an hour or so. Then Captain Cooper shouted, "Let's away from this cesspit, don't make me tell you twice or I'll throttle ye myself and hang you out to dry!"

The crew, shouting and jubilant, scrambled back over to the deck of the *Diana*. Jill crouched by the side, hiding.

Cooper had put a booted foot on the gunwale, ready to cross back to the *Diana* herself, when one of the other crew broke away.

"Take me with you!" the man called, and fell forward, pleading. Really pleading, on his knees, hands clasped and everything. He looked sick, with a long, sallow face and an almost toothless mouth. His hands looked arthritic. But he didn't seem old. "I'll sign your code, I'll scrub your decks, I'll do whatever you say. Take me with you!"

Cooper looked down at him. Still imperious and avenging, she seemed to be considering, but no—she was only taking a moment to sneer at him.

"Keep to the lot you chose, scum." She returned to her ship.

The captain of the slave ship took this moment, when the pirates had already left and he didn't risk retribution, to vent his anger. Sputtering, he clutched the side of his ship with one hand and shook the other, in a fist, at the *Diana*. "God damn you! You're not a woman at all, you're a whore! You're the devil's own whore!"

"Better the devil's than yours!" Marjory Cooper shouted back at him. "Give my regards to your wife!"

With more laughter, the ropes between the two ships were cut, and the *Diana* drifted from her victim.

The crew did the work of setting sail and steering the *Diana* away, quick and smooth, in high spirits. The deck was crowded, because the slaves from the other ship were still there, huddled together, looking furtively around. Maybe wondering if they were in worse danger now than they had been.

Abe passed by Jill on his way to keep watch over the string of prisoners they'd rescued. He glanced at her. "You're frowning."

She was frowning to keep from crying. "I've read about this in books. I mean, everyone knows it happened. But I didn't know . . . I didn't realize . . ."

How could she realize? Compared to this, her life back home was the dream. She wanted to go home.

"You have never had to look it in the face, yes?" She nodded, and his smile turned kind. "That it makes you sad is a good thing." He moved away, to the people in chains.

Captain Cooper was still hollering orders, and Jill still didn't know what to do but watch. Abe said something in another language to one of the prisoners; the man shook his head and pointed to another, who came forward and replied. They had a conversation. Meanwhile, somebody ran forward with a hammer and chisel, and another brought up a big piece of metal—an anvil maybe? The shackles around their feet didn't have keys. They had to be cut open.

Jill couldn't watch, but she couldn't go anywhere on the ship to avoid the noise of it, and the cries of pain.

But they were being set free.

She was about to go belowdecks, to hide away—to stay clear of anyone's attention. There was a shout.

"Tadpole, fetch the surgeon!"

Jill only realized Cooper was talking to her because she was pointing at her. The captain stood near the helm, scrutinizing her. And there was a doctor?

"Surgeon?" she asked.

"The prisoner! Go fetch him!"

That strange, bitter man was a doctor? She had a hard time believing it, but she did what she was told.

Belowdecks, she unbolted the door to his tiny room and said, "You're a doctor?"

The prisoner smirked at her. "Surgeon. What is it, then? Have you stubbed a toe?"

"The captain—"

"Ah yes," he said, sighing, heaving himself from the wall with a great show of effort. "Her majesty the captain has stubbed a toe."

"We captured a slave ship," Jill blurted.

The man's indifferent mask slipped, revealing a moment of disbelief. But the scowl returned. "Bloody hell. That's what all the commotion was, then? Well, let's get on with it." He gestured forward for Jill to lead the way.

She watched the doctor—surgeon—emerge from the hold onto the deck. He squinted into the late afternoon sun, shading his eyes as he regarded the scene. The twenty captives were seated. The crewman with the hammer was still working to free them. Jill could see now that they all had bleeding wounds, either from the shackles or other injuries. The doctor frowned.

No matter where she stood, Captain Cooper was the focus of attention on the ship. No matter what other activity swarmed around her, the woman was easy to find, even if she was standing still, saying nothing. Now the captain was marching toward her and the doctor.

The captain didn't spare Jill a glance, but to the doctor she said, "You'll keep them alive."

"It might be kinder to let them die," the man answered. "I don't know where you plan on setting them ashore, but chances are they'll be captured again and end up worse than they are. Might as well drown them now."

Jill couldn't tell if he was joking. He sounded so harsh.

The captain didn't seem bothered. At least her expression didn't change from its usual hardness. "Treat them as you would any other patient, Mr. Emory, if you please."

"Do you take me for a complete brute?"

"I don't take you for anything," she said, already walking back to the helm.

The doctor stared after her a moment, as if astonished. "Harpy," he muttered. Then he shook his head and got to work. He pointed at Henry. "Boy! Fetch me some water. Fresh from the scuttlebutt mind you, none of that bilge." Henry, hanging from some of the rigging to watch the proceedings, scowled but complied.

Jill continued to stay out of the way and out of notice.

Supper came late that evening, and the rations were slim since a portion of the food was distributed to the new passengers. Jill didn't mind; she wasn't very hungry. The liberated slaves might not have eaten for days, the way they took in the watery soup and hard bread. She could make out ribs on all of them. While eating, they began to smile, and even laugh, almost delirious. Their interpreter spoke to Abe, who answered him as kindly as he'd spoken to her. Jill couldn't imagine what they were thinking.

She'd been feeling sorry for herself ever since that tournament, so upset because she couldn't make a decision about what to do next—but at least she had choices, and a future to go with them. And all she'd done since coming to the *Diana* was complain that she didn't belong here. Well, neither did they. And she hadn't come here in chains. She had nothing to complain about. Nothing. While she still felt trapped here, she suddenly felt lucky.

Well after dark, the new passengers began to sing. The voices were soft, wavering—still weak. Like the lantern light, the words and tunes seemed to rise up among the sails, to echo above them, sounding larger than they were. Jill sat against the side of the ship, near the stern, just out of sight of the small celebration. She didn't want to be seen. But she tipped her head back and stared up, watching the patterns of light and shadow on rippling sails, feeling the vibration as someone pounded a beat on the deck.

When Henry bounded in front of her, dropping from some unseen spot above, she gasped, flinched, and banged her head on the ship's rail. He laughed, taking a cross-legged seat nearby, a shadow just at the edge of the lantern light. His eyes gleamed, like this was all a big party to him.

Rubbing her head, she muttered, "What do you want?"

"I wanted to congratulate you on surviving your first battle," he said.

Frowning, she looked away. That wasn't a battle, it was a raid, a true pirate raid. Or a rescue mission? She'd only watched, dumbstruck. "I didn't do anything."

He shrugged. "You didn't interfere. You didn't make an ass of yourself. Sometimes that's all you can ask for."

That almost sounded like a compliment. "What happens next?"

"I'm guessing we'll sail for Jamaica. There's a place there we can let them off and they'll be safe." He nodded toward the middle of the ship and the group of former slaves. "Some pirates would sell 'em off in Havana, but not us. We may stop somewhere to provision first. However the captain chooses."

None of those plans seemed to offer Jill a way home. But

Captain Cooper wasn't taking her into account—Jill had signed on as crew, hadn't she? She was bound by the captain's articles.

Henry lingered, not smiling this time, not taunting. Just quietly watching her, as if he knew she wanted to talk, which gave her the courage to ask, "Does this happen a lot? Have you done this before?"

"Done what, capture a ship? Of course, plenty of times."

"But a slave ship," she said.

He glanced upward, maybe seeing the same patterns she did. But then he'd probably lived on the ship for years. The view may have seemed ordinary to him. "We try. Because of Abe, you see. It's where he came from. He'd stop every one of those ships sailing from Africa if he could. He'd give up his share of every other haul we make to stop the trade. He can't. But we try."

"What about you?" she said, the question sticking in her throat, because she had a sudden image of Henry, beaten and in chains, and she hated thinking of him like that, however much he might annoy her. It was the opposite of Henry as she saw him now—smiling, bright, fit, alive.

"What about me? Did I come from Africa on a ship like that?" he said, and shrugged. "My mum did, not that she ever talked about it. I was born here, on the islands. Jamaica, in fact."

"And your father?"

He snorted. "Who knows? Some English sailor stopped in port, I reckon. I was bound to turn pirate, wasn't I? A half-breed bastard like me."

He grinned like it was a joke, but she turned away. She wanted to tell him what would happen with the slave trade, how many more decades of suffering were ahead of them, that it would never be made right. But she would sound crazy. Like she was apologizing for a stretch of history she had no control over. But she felt like she ought to apologize.

6

REMISE

Henry was right, and the captain announced that they'd be sailing for Jamaica next. There had been some debate, back and forth, between Captain Cooper and Abe. "We could go east," Abe had said. "Take them home."

Cooper had refused. "We don't have provisions for such a voyage, and we can't be sailing 'cross the Atlantic. Tell them that."

So Abe did, explaining in the language they shared that they couldn't go back home, that they'd be sailing west instead of east. The interpreter seemed to plead with Abe, who relayed the words to Captain Cooper.

"Abe, you know as well as I do we can't take them home," Cooper said. "And we're still going after Blane."

Captain Cooper put it to a vote among the crew—Africa or Jamaica? Only Abe voted for Africa, so they sailed to Jamaica.

Again, Jill watched Captain Cooper holding up the shard of rapier blade, watching it turn on its string, following its length with her gaze to stare out at a different part of the horizon than where they sailed to.

Jill still wondered what the broken rapier meant—how Cooper knew the shard would behave like this, and what the captain hoped to accomplish by following it. And how did Jill fit into that? Or had she been brought here by accident? It was all too strange.

After spending the night on deck, the former slaves went below to continue resting in semidarkness. They were still sick, and the surgeon, Emory, continued to move among them, checking for fevers, dispensing liquid concoctions. Jill hadn't learned anything new about him. He glared at everyone and didn't invite conversation.

The next day, the captain set her to scrubbing the decks again. The whole thing, all over again. When Jill came to the middle of the deck, where the Africans had first been when they came on board, where their irons had been cut off, she found blood. Drops, smears, and stains of it marring the planks. She scraped with the stone, pressing as hard as she could, 'til the muscles in her arms cramped, but she couldn't get the wood clean. Choking up, her throat tightening with tears, she kept scrubbing. She'd clean it, make it shine, if she worked hard enough, scrubbed fast enough.

Startled, she nearly fell over when a hand touched her shoulder. Gasping, Jill saw Captain Cooper standing over her. The pirate's hand rested on her shoulder, then pulled away.

"It's all right, lass. Leave it," she said, and walked away.

Slouching, Jill dropped the stone and watched her go.

Another two days passed.

Jill learned to sail. She learned that the *Diana* was a schooner, and while it might have seemed impressive, it was a speck next to a Spanish treasure galleon or an English ship of the line, or so the sailors told her. She learned about fore-masts and mainmasts, yardarms and rigging, the bowsprit, larboard and starboard, fore and aft. She learned to tie knots and trim sails. At sea, ropes were called lines. She learned the commands that Cooper and Jenks shouted that made the crew scramble like they were a colony of ants, swarming to this sail or that rope—line—and making the changes that caused the ship to speed up, slow down, heave one way or another, plowing the waves in a different direction.

Depending on whether the sails were furled or unfurled, and how, the ship behaved one way and not another. Even if Jill stayed on the ship for years, watching, she wouldn't understand all the details. Many of the crew had, in fact, worked on ships since they were children.

She divided the crew into two camps: the ones who hassled her and the ones who didn't. In the former camp were some of the men from that first day, the ones who harassed her as soon as she came on board—Jenks, John, Martin, and a hulking man the others called Mule, who did much of the heavy lifting. Some of the crew in the second camp ran interference for her: putting themselves between her and the others, butting in before teasing got serious with jokes and laughter of their own. Jill had started to trust some of them—Henry and Abe, and Bessie and Jane, two of the other women on board.

Shrouds were the lines that anchored the masts to the ship. Part of the constant sound of creaking and straining were the tall masts pulling and flexing against the lines. The masts were like the tall trees they'd been made from, always groaning and moving, however slightly, in the constant wind.

The ship had eight cannons on the main deck, locked down and silent for now. Slots in the side of the ship would open and the cannon would be shoved forward if the ship went into battle. Jill wasn't sure she wanted to see a real battle—as opposed to the one-sided raid on the slave ship—but she was curious. She imagined seeing the whole rank of cannons firing would be exciting—as long as she was someplace far away, watching safely through a telescope.

"Have you been in many battles?" she asked Henry at supper, the usual stew of dried meat and potatoes, along with the usual serving of rum. She'd learned to drink it slowly, with plenty of water.

"Of course I have."

"I mean real ones," she said. "Not ones where you run up the black flag and scream and the other ship surrenders without firing a shot. I mean have you ever been shot at."

"Oh, *real* battles," he said, chuckling. "I suppose next you'll be wanting us to fight with honor, all lined up like redcoats."

"I just wondered what it was like," she said.

"It's a lot of fire and a lot of smoke. It's nothing," he said. His smile was bright as ever, but he looked away, hiding a troubled gaze.

They didn't have any battles over the next few days, and they avoided any other encounters. Once or twice the crew on watch shouted out, identifying another ship within view. Usually the other ship was far distant, hard to see, little more than an incongruous shape against the waves. Captain Cooper or Abe would look through the spyglass and call out colors, the patterns of the flags—English or Dutch, sometimes Spanish or French. The captain would order them to sail on, turning to avoid the ship if need be. They sailed fast to their destination.

Jill learned to climb the tall mainmast, hauling herself up on the jungle of lines, and to keep a lookout, tying herself in so she wouldn't fall, eyes squinting against the wind and sun, and to recognize the smudges on the horizon that meant land. They passed islands, small, uncharted, nameless. Captain Cooper seemed to know which ones they were without consulting any maps, which ones had food and water, which provided good harbor, and which were off-limits because other pirates—or worse, some nation's navy—anchored there.

One day, catching sight of the rapier slung on Captain Cooper's belt, Jill realized she hadn't thought about that qualifying tournament, her last bout, and the lost half second in days. She was too busy working, and too tired at night to do anything but sleep in her swaying hammock. She had stopped planning, stopped worrying about what happened next.

It had been far too easy to fall into this life—she was becoming one of them. Someone looking at her from the outside wouldn't be able to tell the difference.

She wondered when she'd finally wake up.

On her second watch, Jill spotted a shape far distant on the water. She thought her eyes were playing tricks, that the light on the water was making her see things. The object seemed to be moving along with the waves, flashing in the sun—light reflecting off sails?

She didn't want to call a warning and be wrong about it—what sort of nickname would that earn her? They didn't think much about learning curves around here; they expected her to just know things she couldn't possibly know. But she watched that spot in the distance for five minutes, rested her eyes by looking around to the horizon and the open water surrounding them, and when she came back to it, the object was still there. It had to be a ship.

"Ahoy!" she called down, as those on watch had done when they saw something. Far below, the captain, Jenks, and others looked up at her—they probably didn't think she knew what she was talking about. "Ship to larboard!" she called, and pointed.

Captain Cooper, identifiable by her coat and fall of auburn hair around her shoulders, went to the port side of the *Diana* and looked through her spyglass. Jill expected her to look a moment, then shout up the mast that she was crazy and seeing things. But Cooper kept staring through the glass.

She put it away with a sense of urgency.

"It's Royal Navy," Cooper said. "Let's get out of their way before they can follow us."

Jill was right, and felt oddly satisfied by it.

Cooper shouted commands for sails to be trimmed, and the ship turned and their speed increased. The movements were subtle. The ship Jill had been watching had come close enough that she could discern the wide hull, three masts, sails, and colored pennants flying from the top of one mast. It might have seen them and started to follow, but the *Diana* skipped away and sped out of view, and the other ship must have decided it was too much trouble to give chase.

When Jill's shift at watch was over and she climbed down the mast, Captain Cooper was waiting for her on deck.

"Good eyes, Tadpole," she said. "The navy patrols are common this close to Port Royal, and it's best we stay out of their way."

Jill didn't want to feel pride, didn't want to feel like she'd just won a touch against a difficult opponent. She wanted to be angry at Cooper for keeping secrets about the rapier shard—and for showing absolutely no interest in getting Jill home. She definitely didn't want to get used to being here. But she did feel pride, and she was getting used to it.

The sun set on another day.

"We'll careen her once we pull into the cove," the captain announced the next morning. "It'll take time to get everyone sorted, might as well take advantage."

Land had come into view, a looming shape of island larger than many others they'd encountered, but not as large as Hispaniola or Cuba, which they'd slid past without approaching. This was Jamaica, their destination.

Jenks shouted orders, and the *Diana* changed direction, veering away before they'd drawn close enough to even make out trees and hills on the landmass.

"We want to stay out of the way," Henry said, noting Jill's confusion. "Port Royal's south, and more trouble than we want just now."

While they never left sight of the island, they didn't draw any closer until late in the afternoon. They'd furled sails and tacked slowly into a western wind, making little progress. But Cooper stood on the foredeck, brass spyglass to her eye, searching for something. Once, she handed it to Abe, who called out and pointed.

Their port was deceptive. Jill would have sworn they sailed toward a solid piece of land, but as they drew closer, she saw that it was a separate island, long and thin, with beaches and palm trees, but no more than thirty feet wide. They rounded it, sailing into an inlet, calm and narrow, between the slender island and a corner of the Jamaican coast.

Jill's heart sank. When they reached land, she'd assumed there'd be a town, some kind of civilization. Then she could escape—and do what? She still didn't know. She'd still be stuck a long way from home.

"Where's the port?" Jill said. She stood at the side with Henry to watch the ship's approach to land.

The captain overheard. "And have us all caught and hanged? The big ships can't get in here, and the spit of land'll hide us. We can stay here long as we like."

Jill said, "But I was hoping . . . I thought—"

"Thought what?" Cooper said.

"If we're in a city, I'd have a better chance of finding my way home."

"You signed articles, you're crew now. This is your home."

"But—"

"That's enough of that." Cooper walked off, and Jill had to leave the argument there.

The empty beach drew closer and closer, until a shudder passed through the hull, and the ship listed, then didn't move at all. Jill grabbed a rope to keep from falling over. They'd run the *Diana* aground.

Then the work began. Dozens of sailors moved cannons

on their wooden frames, securing them all to the port side of the ship, which, with all the weight on one side, began leaning sharply. Abe gathered the African passengers together and handed them ropes, gesturing them over the side. Emory, the doctor—surgeon, rather, though Jill hadn't quite figured out the difference—was brought up on deck, squinting in the bright sun and beach, looking bedraggled in an untucked shirt, trousers, and scuffed shoes. One of the men tried to hand him a crate to carry to shore. Emory sneered and crossed his arms. After that, people ignored him. Even though he was a prisoner, no one bothered locking him up. But it wasn't like he had anywhere to go. Just like Jill.

While she was watching, listening to the ominous creaks and groans the ship was making, Jenks came at her with a load of rope and pulleys. He was struggling to stay upright on the now steeply leaning deck—Jill herself didn't dare let go of her handhold.

"You! Tadpole!"

Jill wished that name hadn't stuck.

Jenks stumbled up beside her and leaned on the mast. "Take these to the beach." He started transferring coils of ropes from his shoulder to hers; she scrambled to grab hold of them without letting them drop into a tangled mess. Square wooden pulleys, block and tackle, banged against her. The gear looked heavy when he'd been handling it. She thought she was going to fall over under the load.

"What's happening?" she asked.

"Don't you know anything?" He marched off, shaking his head.

They were wrecking the ship—but she had to trust the pirates wouldn't do such a thing. No one else seemed to be panicking. And as usual, they were happy to give her jobs to do without explaining how to do them. She heaved her load more firmly onto her shoulder, looked around, and aimed for Abe, who had one foot propped on the side of the ship, keeping balance as he helped the last of the Africans off the ship.

Then she let go. Leaning back against the slope, she let gravity pull her along, half trotting toward the side. She concentrated on standing upright; she could see herself falling, pulleys knocking into her, rope tangling her up as she rolled along. Then the crew would come up with a better name than Tadpole for her.

Abe saw her and paused to cross his arms and grin as she slammed into the side.

"Where you going with all that?" he said.

"Jenks said take it to the beach."

"Here." He took hold of the coils and lifted them off her. Gratefully, she extricated her arms from the tangle.

With more strength and ability than she would have managed, he swung the gear, putting his whole body, broad shoulders and muscular arms, into the move, and threw them over. They fell on a clear spot on the beach.

"That makes it easier, yes?" Abe said, his smile teasing. "Go on, you're next."

Leave it to Jenks not to tell her the easy way to do a job.

Everyone was disembarking. Abe handed her a line—and she went for it. Holding on to the rope dangling from the mast, she jumped over the side and looked down to see frothing waves under her. She was smart enough not to slide—the rough rope would have taken off her skin—but instead lowered herself hand over hand. With a few feet left to go, she let go and dropped into the water, sending up a splash.

Above her, Abe cheered, "That's it, Tadpole! Soon you'll be a proper frog!"

She smiled back at him. After the hot days on the ship, the just-cool-enough water swirling around her legs felt wonderful. She stood there for a moment, enjoying it.

Then it was time to get back to work.

Most of the crew landed on the beach in the next half hour, with more armloads of ropes and pulleys, which began to come together in a mechanism. They rigged a pulley system between the ship and a couple of tall, strong palm trees on the beach. When that was in place, they used it to lower cannons off the ship. Jill watched in awe as part of the crew worked to lower six of the huge metal guns to the sand, and another part piled up mounds of sand to mount them on. The remaining two stayed on board as counterweights. They turned the beach into a miniature fort, with cannons resting on mounds of sand, facing outward, toward the water and any ships that might be foolish enough to approach. Jill helped dig when Henry handed her a shovel and pointed.

The *Diana* rested at a steep angle, her hull exposed, especially now that the tide was going out.

Henry seemed pleased at Jill's awe at the whole process. He joined her while she stood on the beach, staring. "When the tide's out, we'll start cleaning," he said.

"Cleaning?"

"Scrubbing the hull. Don't worry, you'll get to help— you should be good at scrubbing by now."

He led her down the beach and a few steps into the water, until the sloping hull of the *Diana* came into view. The part that was always underwater was black, slick with slime, dripping with fronds of seaweed, and jagged with barnacles.

"We have to clean *that*?" she said, despairing. And she'd thought the deck was bad.

"Three times a year or the hull would rot through."

So. They cleaned the hull.

A dozen of them, led by Abe, climbed back aboard the *Diana*. Literally, since it was now impossible to simply walk across the deck. They anchored themselves to the side with ropes and made their way down the sloping hull. A few went first with steel blades and rakes, scraping off barnacle shells, which cracked and oozed over the wood, dripping into the water below, turning the wooden surface into a slippery, gooey mess. A few of the others, Jill among them, followed with brushes and brooms. Scrubbing the deck had meant polishing something that was already mostly clean, removing a film of salt water and daily wear. This was completely different. A salty, rotting stench rose up from the slime that they scraped, shoved, and swept back into the sea. Some of the others tied scarves over their mouths; Bessie gave Jill a blue square of cloth so she could do the same. The scarf over her mouth made it hard to breathe; the air she took in was hot, stifling. It was a trade-off—which was worse, not being able to breathe well, or smelling the full force of the rot they peeled off sixty feet of hull? She kept the scarf on.

The water immediately around the ship turned cloudy, filled with debris. Small fish and crabs swam in, darting back and forth, nibbling on bits of barnacle and seaweed.

When she started, Jill was still sore and tired from days of scrubbing the deck. Then she stopped thinking about being tired at all as her movements became mechanical. This was only one side. They still had to roll the ship over and do the other side. She'd have to tell Tom and Mandy how much time pirates spent cleaning. They'd never believe it.

Assuming she ever saw them again and got to tell them anything. She never thought she'd miss them so much.

They didn't finish that day. The sun set, the sky grew dark, and the hull still had to be examined and damages repaired. That couldn't be done by the shadowy, flickering light from the fires and torches lit onshore.

The evening routine went on the same as it did on the ship, except dinner included fresh fruit—mangos, papayas, and others that Jill had never seen before, incredibly tart and juicy, so full of flavor they almost burned her tongue. She'd never tasted fruit like this, so fresh, eaten moments after being picked. It made her ration of rum and water taste smoother, brighter. So this was where rum punch came from.

The group of freed slaves stayed together at the edge of the camp, sharing a flask of water and eating food. They had started talking among themselves more, as if waking up, coming out of a nightmare. They looked around with wondering gazes and seemed content to sit in the open air. Among the pirates, they only ever talked to Abe.

The doctor also sat alone, watching the proceedings,

not showing any inclination to run away—because where would he go?

Captain Cooper set watches, guards to look for lights and listen for the sound of ships on the water, or anyone approaching from the interior of the island. Watches on land seemed more tense, more fraught than they did on the water. At sea, anything that approached was visible for miles; nothing could surprise them, and they could run in any direction. Here, they were stuck. There were far too many ways to approach them in secret, and not enough ways to flee. And Jill worried along with the rest of them, no matter how much she told herself she didn't feel safe with the *Diana*'s crew, that she didn't care. They weren't *her* people, she didn't belong here, she didn't feel any loyalty to them. Let the Royal Navy catch them—even Henry—then she could run away. But that wouldn't work, either, because Emory was right. As far as everyone was concerned, she *was* one of them. And she didn't want to get arrested, captured, hanged, or any of the other possible nightmares. So she worried.

The captain assigned Jill to a turn standing watch. More looking out over the water, searching for enemies that might or might not appear as phantoms in the distance. It was a wonder they didn't all go blind, doing this day after day.

She went out to a spit of land, a sandbar extending from

the natural harbor, and found the trunk of a fallen palm to sit on. If she didn't fall asleep, she'd consider her job done. Not seeing anything dangerous come along needing her to raise an alarm would be a bonus.

Back at the camp on the beach, some of the pirates were still awake, singing and drinking in the shelter of the campfire's light. They made Jill grouchy; they'd spent all day working their butts off, they ought to be exhausted. How could they be happy here?

Resting her chin on her palm, she stared out over the water, which hadn't changed at all. It still went on forever, still rippled with endless waves, the same waves she watched back at Nassau, when everything was normal. Now, though, they were flecked silver by the moonlight. Then there were the stars—tipping back her head, she looked up past the palm fronds, past the thin smoke from the fire, and saw a sky bright with stars. The scene was hypnotizing. Staying awake ended up being a big enough challenge in its own right. She'd never been so sore, and she didn't imagine there was a hot tub around to soak the aches away. She could fall asleep watching the waves, dreaming of hot water and cold sodas. She'd never complain about homework again.

Outside the circle of the camp's fire, the world was mostly shades of blue, black, and silver. Cool colors, soft and restful. A flicker of yellow at the edges of Jill's vision caught her attention. She straightened, squinting to better see it. It flashed again on the other side of the cove, like a bit of flame in midair. Past the camp, past the ship, at the very edges of the trees, on the shore looking out over the ocean.

A lantern, she thought. Someone there was holding a lantern.

7

REDOUBLEMENT

She almost shouted, but stopped herself. Her call would carry over the water, and whoever was holding the lantern would escape before anyone reached the spot. Jill jumped from her perch and ran as well as she could, sliding in the sand, following the edge of the forest.

"Tadpole?" Abe said as she came around behind the camp.

"There's someone with a lantern out there," she said. Abe got up and signaled, and he and a couple of the pirates followed her, pistols in hand.

As she reached the end of the cover, the light was still

there, and she could see the figure of the man holding the lantern.

It was Emory, the surgeon. She recognized his silhouette by the shape of his clothes and the rough cut of his hair.

"Hey," she said.

Quickly, he turned around and slammed closed the shutter on the lantern.

"Signaling your navy friends, eh?" Abe said, and he didn't sound surprised. He might even have been amused.

Emory straightened. Jill couldn't see his expression clearly but imagined him frowning. "You can't slip by them forever. They'll find you, eventually, and you'll all hang."

"Get on with you, back to camp," Abe said. The two others grabbed the surgeon by the arms and led him along, pulling him so that he stumbled. "Good eyes again, Tadpole," Abe said to her.

Jill didn't feel any better. She spent a moment looking out to the horizon and didn't see anything, no sign that Emory was signaling anyone in particular rather than randomly flashing the light in the hope that someone spotted him.

Back at the camp, Abe tied Emory's hands and feet and left him sitting sullenly near the fire. Then he told Jill to get some rest.

Hard to do when Emory slumped against a barrel, glowering at her where she sat in the sand with a thin blanket she'd dug out of the pile of gear from the ship. Jill had the feeling that the crew wouldn't have bothered keeping him around at all except his skills as a surgeon were too valuable to let go. But it seemed like more trouble than it was worth. Except the alternative was probably not just letting him go, but tipping him over the side. That didn't seem right, either.

"So you've thrown your lot in with them for certain," he said to her in a low voice that didn't carry. "We could have helped each other."

"You're not helping much of anyone," she muttered.

"What is your name—Tadpole?" She scowled and he chuckled. "Your pardon. It's Miss Jill, isn't it? You don't belong here. I can see that."

At least someone could.

The others were scattered along the beach, lying stretched out or curled up, snoring, sleeping off the rum, dead to the world after the day of hard work.

"Where are you from, really?" he said.

Shaking her head, she gave a wry smile. "A long way from here."

"Philadelphia? Boston?" he said. "Or did you cross the Atlantic to get here?"

There was no point explaining it.

"Jill, the Royal Navy will find us, sooner or later. They'll take the ship and everyone aboard her prisoner. But if you help me, I can save you. I can get you a pardon."

"Help you, how?"

"Untie me, and we can both escape. Lead the navy here ourselves and collect the bounty on the pirates," he said.

"Escape and go where?" she whispered. They were in wilderness. The jungle and hills were a solid wall around them.

"We follow the coast. It's easy." He sounded desperate and unbelievable.

She was absolutely sure that Emory didn't care anything about her, only about getting what he wanted. He'd use her and she might or might not get a pardon out of it. At least Cooper and the others seemed to care about her, so long as she was part of the crew anyway.

"If I untied you, what do you think the captain would do to me?"

They both knew the answer: killed, marooned, both. Emory said, "She wouldn't, not to you. Not to another female."

Like that would make any difference to Captain Cooper. Jill moved away to spread her blanket on her own patch of sand, to try to sleep.

But she thought about what he'd said. Getting captured by the Royal Navy would certainly be one way of getting out of here. But it wouldn't get her any closer to home. She could almost sympathize with Emory, though. This was a strange place for him, too. But his path was so much clearer.

Though exhausted, Jill had trouble sleeping in the open, on a sandy bed in a deserted cove. Wrapping the blanket around herself, she curled up in a warm pocket of sand. The air grew surprisingly cool, even in the tropics, as a breeze blew in from the ocean. She wished for a room and a bed. She was never going to get all the sand out of her hair.

Sleep came in fits and starts. The ground kept moving under her, starting her awake. But no, it was only the phantom movement of the schooner's rocking that her muscles still braced against. Her arms were numb, dead from the endless work of scraping the hull. The blisters and sore muscles were a solid ache. Her head hurt even worse when she closed her eyes. What kind of life was this? How could the others sing and laugh every night? And the waves never quieted, continually rustling, nudging Jill back into consciousness.

Then the watch shouted an anxious hail—someone was coming. In the shadows of the campfire, wavering against the wall of trees and vegetation at the edge of the beach, silhouettes appeared, human shapes emerging to stand in the open.

"Captain!" the man on watch shouted again. More of the crew awoke; their agitated murmurs grew louder.

"Settle down," Cooper answered. Unlike the others, she didn't sound sleepy or worried. The woman's figure joined the wavering shadows. She was upright, fully dressed, moving quickly, as if she'd never gone to sleep. Maybe she hadn't.

A dozen people—lithe, dark-skinned—had emerged from the trees. Jill recognized their stances, the way they moved—wary, like they were ready for a fight. They held weapons in front of them—swords with short, thick blades. Machetes, maybe. Some of them held long shotguns—muskets, rather. The firelight burnished them and their weapons to a shade of copper.

The captain faced the new arrivals and said, "Nanny?"

One of the shadows stepped forward—a woman, her hair bound tight to her head; wiry, with powerful limbs, wearing a long skirt and a full blouse. She was shorter than the walking staff she leaned on, but could surely use the length of wood as a weapon. She held it as if she could raise and swing it in a moment.

"Marjory," the woman said in a low voice that carried over the beach. "You bring trouble."

"I know, Nanny. I'm sorry for it," the captain said, and Jill was shocked to hear the deference in her voice. Captain

Cooper didn't defer to anyone. She might have been the strongest person Jill had ever met—but Jill wondered if maybe this Nanny was the strongest person Marjory Cooper had ever met.

"Tell me the story," Nanny said in a broad, round accent. The woman gestured to the central fire, still burning low in its pit of sand. Cooper led Nanny to it, and they sat in its light.

The others who had come with Nanny stayed around the perimeter of the camp, keeping a lookout.

Jill watched the two women at the fire. She didn't dare approach, though she was fascinated. But now she couldn't even try to sleep, so she sat up, wrapped in her blanket, and watched.

"We raided a ship of slavers," Cooper said. "Abe and me raided it—you know how it is. We couldn't take them back home so we brought them here. It's the only safe place for them, Nanny. I know you won't turn them away."

"You take advantage of my hospitality. We've all escaped, we all fight every day to keep the freedom we won. There are still hunters from the plantations crawling through these trees looking for us. How am I supposed to hide all these folk? And how we going to feed so many new mouths?"

"You'll find a way. We've got some stores on the ship we can give you. But I know you won't let me take these folk to the market in Havana."

The woman chuckled, a rich, sly sound. "Oh, you won't do that, or you would have already. I know you, Marjory."

The captain looked away, just for a moment.

Nanny said, "Let me meet them, speak to them."

The group of Africans was still at their own camp a little way off from the others, away from the work, the fire, and the pirates. But they had not left; Jill had expected them to just walk away. Nothing was keeping them from leaving—except the jungle and the unknown. The same reason Emory had tried to signal a ship rather than simply walk away.

Jill supposed she could walk away, except that she still didn't know exactly where she was, still didn't have any idea how to fend for herself, how to get food or water, and she didn't know how to get back home. So maybe she did understand them, a little. But then she didn't have sores around her ankles like they did, from where the shackles had bound them, so maybe she didn't understand at all.

Nanny went to the group and spoke in a different language. One of them answered her, and a conversation began. Occasionally one of the others would speak up—and the first one who'd spoken would seem to repeat, but with different words. They didn't all speak the same language, and maybe Nanny didn't speak the same languages that Abe did. Nanny asked questions, and the one who understood her answered. Even though Jill didn't understand what they were saying, she stayed awake, listening to the voices lilting like music.

Captain Cooper remained standing nearby, watching. She sent her own crew to sleep, so Nanny's people were the only ones keeping watch.

The sky had begun to pale when the conversation stopped, and Nanny turned back to Cooper. "You are a pirate," Nanny said to Cooper.

"So you say," the captain answered, tired. "What does that make you?"

"A young woman getting old," Nanny said. "Your orphans, I'll take them home with me, like you knew I would."

"Thank you," Cooper said, and seemed relieved.

"But you owe me," Nanny said, pointing with the staff.

"Put it on my account, woman."

The camp began to wake, the fires were fed, voices murmured with greetings of the morning. Jill watched, dazed, still in a dream. When she woke up, she'd be in her own bed, in the modern world, where she belonged.

Nanny had moved off to talk to one of her guards, and the Africans were standing, stretching, as if getting ready for a walk. Captain Cooper came toward Jill.

"Have you been up all night, listening in on us?" the captain said, looking down on Jill with a furrowed brow and a quirked smile. Jill nodded meekly. The captain shook her head. "You're such a tadpole."

Jill certainly felt small at the moment.

"Get up, then," Cooper said. "There's a group going inland for fresh water. You'll go with them."

Jill was tired of work, sweat and dirt, blisters on her hands, and not understanding what was happening. But following orders was easier than arguing. She picked herself up, stretched, tried to brush some of the sand off, and didn't succeed.

Every new job she was given was worse than the last. Nanny's people told them that there was a creek with clear, fresh water just a little ways into the forest. The mouth of it was up the shore half a mile. All they had to do was get one of the rowboats, row the barrels there, fill them up, and bring them back.

The barrels were as big as Jill. She could hide inside one if she scrunched up. While others continued scrubbing the hull, Jill helped wrestle the empty water barrels up from the hold, lower them into one of the rowboats, and row to the mouth of the stream, which was narrow, rocky, and crowded with overhanging branches and foliage. The others made her the guinea pig, testing the water every few yards, tasting handfuls of it until it turned fresh. She must have spit out a dozen mouthfuls of briny, mucky water. Then, when they finally reached fresh water that hadn't been tainted by the tide rolling in from the coast, they had to fill the barrels, load them back in the rowboat, and return to the shore to load the barrels back on the *Diana*.

She hadn't understood the phrase "backbreaking work" until the last couple of days. She was beginning to think she'd never done any work at all. She'd had an easy life, wandering on the beach on vacation; she wanted to go back to her easy life.

She had tied her hair up with a scarf to keep sweat from running into her eyes. Her clothing was soaked with it. She was so hot, she only wanted to run into the water and float there, rocked gently by the waves. After helping to guide the rowboat back to the ship, Jill rested at the edge of the sand, catching her breath, feeling the sweat drip off her in rivers. Her face was red and burning.

She didn't notice that she had stopped next to Nanny, who was watching her, head tilted with curiosity, suppressing a smile.

"You look terrible, girl," the woman said. Jill nearly cried. She might have whimpered.

"And what's your story?" Nanny said, leaning on her staff. "Has Marjory found her apprentice to be the next pirate queen?"

Jill shook her head. "I don't even think she likes me."

At that, Nanny smiled wide. "Sit down here in the shade. Marjory won't care if you rest a moment."

Nanny moved to the edge of the foliage, in a spot of cool shade, and sat cross-legged. She waved Jill over, and Jill followed. The shade felt blissful. She closed her eyes to rest them.

"So, where are you from?" Nanny asked. "No real pirate would row a boat like you did, splashing the water all about."

Jill sighed. "I'm from a long way away."

Nanny furrowed her brow and said, "Just how far?"

Maybe because she was a stranger, a disinterested third party without a hold on her, Jill told her everything. Not just the boat tour from the modern Bahamas, falling overboard, and being pulled out by the unlikely Captain Cooper and her crew. But even before then, her frustration with her family, with herself, with her fencing and not qualifying for the world championships by half a second. And the realization that if she didn't have fencing, she didn't know what she had, or who she was. She didn't know why she was here. She was adrift with strangers on a wide ocean.

She finished, rubbing her hand over her gritty hair, staring out at waves crawling up the beach a dozen yards away, at the blue morning sky. Her eyes stung, but she hadn't cried. She felt wrung out and tired, though. Like now that she'd told the story, told everything, she was empty. Ready to be filled up by sun, wind, and waves.

"Captain Cooper seems to think it's all tied up in that broken piece of sword," Jill said, and sighed. "But as far as she's concerned it's not about me, it's about this Blane guy."

"Yes. Edmund Blane. Your captain—"

"She's not my captain."

Nanny raised a brow and gave her a look. Jill shut up. "Your captain has good reason to hate him and will fight him if she can. If she thinks you have a way for her to get to Blane—she'll keep you close. You and that bit of sword."

"Can that little piece really find him?" Jill said.

"I think—I think the sword will want to be whole again."

"And will that help me get back home?"

Dark eyes shining in a shadowed, sculpted face, Nanny shifted her grip on her staff and looked out at the sea and the crew still scrubbing the hull of *Diana*, and the others working on the beach, slow but steady. Her expression remained wry.

"Sometimes you can't go back. These people, these stolen slaves, maybe they go back someday. Probably not. So you go forward instead. Don't find your place in the world, make your place. I was a girl, stolen from home in Africa. I still dream of going back. But here, I have a calling, taking care of these people. I can't argue that. Maybe you'll get back to where you came from, but is it really home?"

Jill wiped her eyes, which were threatening tears again.

From the hills deep within the forest, the sudden noise of barking dogs sounded. Activity on the beach stopped a moment.

Nanny looked up and frowned. Planting her staff, she used it to pull herself to her feet. "We've got to move."

"What is it?"

"Plantation foremen's hounds tracking us." She called out to her people.

Jill stood, gingerly straightening cramped muscles and aching joints. "What if they find you?"

She chuckled. "They won't find us."

"But what if they come here?"

"Oh, they won't mess with Marjory's crew. Good luck to you."

"Thanks."

"And if Marjory asks you to be her pirate queen apprentice, tell her no. That girl is trouble."

If Jill hadn't been so exhausted, she might have laughed. Nanny squeezed her arm with her calloused, bony hand, and strode across the beach where her people had gathered. The Africans stood with them, stretching their muscles, looking into the jungle with a mix of hope and trepidation.

At least they had hope. Abe stood by and waved a farewell as they trekked into the trees, and away.

The work went on.

That night at suppertime, the crew gathered around the fire, and everyone moaned and complained about sore muscles and blisters. Some of the crew had gone hunting and killed one of the feral pigs that roamed the jungle, and they celebrated the good roast meat. Even Jill enjoyed the fresh food, though she wasn't happy seeing the pig butchered. She decided she preferred fresh meat that came wrapped in plastic.

When she had her tin plate of food and mug of rum, she found Henry and sat near him.

Jill leaned close and spoke softly, "Why does Captain Cooper have it in for Edmund Blane? What happened?"

Henry glanced at her. "How much have you heard already?"

"Nothing, really. The captain hates him, from the way she talks about him. I didn't know his whole name until Nanny told me."

He chuckled. "Grandy Nanny is a right fierce woman, isn't she?"

"How does Captain Cooper know her?"

"Not sure, it was before my time. But I know there's a story there. Nanny was a slave on a plantation, but escaped.

She's been helping others do likewise ever since. You say her name in Kingston, and the white folk'll curse you down the street."

"She sounds like a hero to me," Jill said.

He shrugged. "We don't get to decide who the heroes are, do we?"

He was right, she supposed. "What about Blane?"

Henry watched the fire a moment and took a drink of rum. "He's evil. He's the kind of pirate that other pirates despise. How's that for a hated man?"

"What's he done?" Jill asked.

"What hasn't he? Burned, destroyed, raped, looted. He'll give a ship quarter, then slaughter everyone aboard. I don't know what exactly he did to our Captain Cooper, but I do know they started a voyage on the same boat, and when it ended he had the boat and she was a castaway."

However Jill felt about Captain Cooper, even that shred of story made her angry at Blane on Cooper's behalf.

"If he's so bad, how does he even get a crew to sign on with him?" Jill asked.

"Because some men like the kind of power he has. It's like they hope it'll brush off on them. But they'll end up worse than the folk we rescued off that slave ship."

"And Captain Cooper wants to take revenge on him."

"I expect so."

"What'll she do when she finds him?"

"Oh, that's an easy one. She'll try to kill him. We're all headed for a battle with him and his ship. We followed him to the *Newark*, where we found you—and nothing but wreckage. Then he got away from us."

The singing started again, and the drinking progressed in earnest until Jill could smell the rum on the air. Captain Cooper, out for revenge, was apart, perched on a barrel, looking to the sea, as if she could find Blane just by staring at the horizon.

And what did any of it have to do with Jill?

Maybe you'll get back. . . . And what if she didn't? She couldn't think like that—she'd get home somehow. Because she wanted to get home—to get back to her life. She missed her old life, she realized, all of it. But that meant she had to stop sitting around, just another member of the crew, waiting. If they were heading for a fight with Blane, she had to be ready.

Jill said, "I can fight, you know. I am a fighter."

"What?"

"When we boarded the other ship, you said I'm not a fighter. But I am, even though no one fights for real anymore where I come from. At least not with swords. But I can."

"You're not. You've never drawn blood."

"Have you?" she countered. "You didn't exactly do any

fighting on the slave ship. Is it really a battle if no one actually hits anyone?"

"You can't deny us the victory."

She couldn't, but it still seemed like something other than a battle. Then again, they were pirates, not the navy.

"Let's practice," she said. She had blisters on her hands and her arms still ached from all the work. Despite all that, she itched to show him that she did know how to fight. At least, she thought she could.

"Practice?" he said.

"Yeah. How else am I going to get good enough to draw blood?"

He seemed to consider her a moment—maybe deciding whether or not to treat her request as a joke. Then, he smiled. "Don't want to stand around and miss out on the fun next time, eh? When we meet Blane, maybe?"

"Maybe I just want to hold a sword again." Prove to herself that she still could. Prove that the bout in the tournament was a fluke, and that she could fight. If not back home, then here.

"Fair enough. And you have a good arm, I remember. All right, then. Tomorrow, first thing in the morning, before the sun gets too high and before Jenks or Abe gets on us for slacking our work."

8

ALLEZ

Exhausted, Jill slept well that night and woke with a start at first light, wondering if Henry would go through with the practice he'd promised her. She hadn't held a sword in weeks, and she missed it. She was surprised—but pleased.

She got up, drank a mug of water, rinsed her face and hands, and looked around. Most of the rest of the crew weren't up yet. The surgeon was awake, sitting with his back propped against a crate, his hands still bound before him. Captain Cooper wasn't around at all.

Henry, however, was coming toward her from the pile of

ship stores that had been brought onto the beach while the *Diana* was careened. He held a sword in each hand.

She smiled for the first time in what must have been weeks.

They stood face-to-face, *en garde*. Jill kept shifting her feet in the soft sand, and nervously rearranging her hold on the grip. Fidgeting. A beginner's mistake. She could feel every one of the muscles in her arm. She watched Henry, expecting him to jump at her, and wondering if she'd be able to do anything but scramble out of the way. Was she out of practice or just nervous?

"You've only ever used practice swords. Baited blades. Right?"

She nodded.

"You've got to stand tall. You've got to be just as bold with a real sword as you are in practice."

She wanted to say that she was bold, she was confident, she knew how to use a sword. But he was right—the sharp edge made her cautious. He'd seen her fidgeting, nervous. While this might be practice, if she screwed up she'd slice him open. He could slice *her* open without meaning to. She didn't know that she trusted him not to slice her open by accident. She was pretty sure she didn't trust herself not to screw up.

At least they had a doctor on hand.

"Really," he said, "all you've got to do is the same things you've always done, but with live steel in your hands. You may not think there'd be any difference, but there is. It makes you careful. Now, let's start with parrying."

He didn't jump at her, didn't tease her. He drilled with her, slowly and carefully. Straightening his arm, he thrust his rapier toward her, not coming close enough to strike. She could parry—blocking his blade with her own as she took a short step back. Then riposting—thrusting toward him while his sword was off target. Again, not coming close enough to strike. She felt stupid, like a beginner starting all over again. But he was right; this was a different sword, and she needed to retrain her muscles. The only way to do that was to practice the basic moves. Learning how the sword felt, learning how to use it, practicing so that it would go where she guided it, stop when she wanted it to stop. Strike when she wanted it to strike and not a moment later.

They advanced and retreated, following one another back and forth across the beach, kicking up sand as they went, until she wasn't sure who was leading and who was following, whether he was directing the drill or she was. They both pretended to attack; they both blocked. She learned to anticipate and evade; then he'd step it up a notch. They were nearly moving at speed. But the precision, the

126

control of their movements—it never stopped being practice—calmed her. *This*, she knew. Her muscles understood it more than scrubbing decks and hulls. Her mind forgot about being on an island in the middle of the ocean, a million miles from everything, the strangeness, the slave ship—this whole world.

Her skin grew sticky with sweat, her hair sticking to it, so that she had to pause to wipe her face on her sleeve. She'd have rather not stopped at all.

She backed off and lowered her sword to signal the break. Chest working as she caught her breath, she scrubbed her cheeks on her shoulder. She smelled like salt and sweat and badly needed a shower—not that she'd seen a real shower in weeks.

Henry had bent over, letting his sword hang loose in his hand and leaning on his knees. His mouth was open in a wide grin, and he had to pause between words. "That's bloody brilliant. Been ages since anyone's given me a go like that!"

People were shouting. They'd collected an audience. Sailors had gathered in a circle around where Jill and Henry had been practicing. Now that the fighters looked up, their audience was raising fists and voices, cheering, like they'd been putting on a show.

"How's that, eh? They think you're pretty good!" Henry

straightened and slapped a hand on her shoulder. She was so tired she nearly fell over, but she managed a smile.

Captain Cooper had moved to a place at the front of the crowd and seemed to study her with a narrowed gaze. Jill couldn't tell if she approved or not. Then Cooper turned back, walked away, and people closed in behind her.

Someone put a mug in Jill's hand. She could smell it without bringing it to her face—rum, of course, mixed with something fruity, lime juice maybe. She'd rather have had a bottle of Gatorade, but she drank it anyway. At least she'd be getting some vitamins.

After that, in addition to working on the ship, Jill and Henry practiced every day. He taught her new tricks—like not fighting in a straight line. "In a real fight," he said, "You're not going to stand in the same place. Your opponent won't stand in the same place while you move back and forth like toys. You've got to go 'round, ducking and dodging. You might be on sand or rock or the deck of a sinking ship. You've got to go anywhere." He sprang to the top of a barrel, balancing there, nearly causing her heart to stop because he was only a step away from falling. But he didn't. He cut the air a couple of times, and sprang away to a set of crates, which he used as a shield. "This is real fighting!" he said, laughing.

As if all the hundreds of bouts she'd fought at her fencing tournaments weren't real. But he was right; they weren't. A fight for a medal wasn't anything like a fight for life and death. Until now, all her fights had referees and rules about scoring, about what parts of the body you could hit. All with baited blades with no edge. Here, their only spectators were pirates hoping to see blood.

Then he gave her a dagger and showed her how to fight with two weapons at once.

"Where did you learn all this?" she asked him. They'd taken a break, rinsing off in the waves before sitting in the shade. Chores waited for them; she was delaying the inevitable.

"Now, that's a story," he said, leaning against one of the stacked barrels. "It was a pair of Englishmen, naval officers stationed at the fort at Port Royal. They did it as a joke at first, thinking, here's this scrawny mulatto kid hanging about, wants to play with swords. Thing is, they didn't expect me to keep coming back for more. I found myself a rapier—"

"Found, or stole?" Jill said, lips curled in a smile.

He tipped his head, conceding the point. "All right, I *acquired* one. Learned as much as I could convince them to teach me. Practiced all I could. Started picking fights. I knew I was getting good when people started placing bets on me. Then I put to sea thinking I could find my fortune, like lots of blokes. Haven't done too badly, I think. I'm not starving and I'm not in chains."

Those were pretty low standards, Jill thought. But around here they didn't exactly have the Olympics to aspire to. "And that's it? You're a pirate for the rest of your life? Fight duels until you go up against someone better than you?"

"I just have to make sure that never happens, right?" he said.

A fraction of a second, she thought. It could happen to anyone.

The work would never be over. They'd cleaned one side of the hull; then they needed to clean the other. Moving the ship took almost a full day and involved rearranging the rigging, untying countless knots and reassembling winches and pulleys. Part of the crew climbed on board the listing ship to shift weights. They waited until the tide came in; the ship floated again; then with a great heave, and much of the crew pulling on ropes, they rolled her over. The tide went out again, exposing a fresh expanse of barnacle and slime-crusted wood. Once again, Jenks called for them to start scraping. Jill nearly cried. Her hands were chapped and bleeding. Rough rope had left splinters of fiber in her skin. All of it stung when she washed her hands in seawater, but the stinging was better than the aching, simply because it was a change.

It was only slightly heartening that many others of the crew also groaned and whined. "You want your shares, you get up on the hull and pull your bleeding weight!" Captain Cooper hollered.

"What shares?" Jenks muttered. "We ain't hauled ourselves a prize in weeks, since you wouldn't sell that last lot!" Grumbling murmurs supported him. Jill needed a moment to realize they were talking about the Africans.

She also would have sworn that Cooper was on the other side of the ship, far up the beach, totally out of earshot, and that she couldn't possibly have heard. But there she was, as if she'd been coming this way on a different purpose, just in time to hear the dissent. Without hesitation the pirate captain shouted back, "You keep talking like that, you mangy hound, and I'll sell *you* in the Carolinas next time we sail that way. Don't think I need you on this ship!"

Jenks didn't have a response for that, but he was still muttering to himself when he grabbed hold of a rope to haul himself up the side of the hull. The threat sounded like just a threat, but by the way the men reacted, Jill had to wonder if such a punishment had happened before. And she wondered how much trouble she'd have to get into before the captain decided to sell her off in the Carolinas.

That didn't bear thinking on.

Scraping the port side of the hull wasn't any less gross or smelly than the starboard side had been. Jill thought about doing this three times a year, every year, with endless days of sailing in between. The only dubious reward for it all seemed to be the rum at the end of the day. And the stars over the ocean at night.

They'd been onshore a week and were on their second day of cleaning the other side of the hull. Nanny and her people had left four days before, and Jill and Henry had been practicing all that time. Jill was almost proud of the work, of being able to see the actual planks of wood and layer of tar that made up the hull and had been hidden by all the gunk. Maybe she was only relieved that it was almost over.

She was on the shore, helping coil line and waiting for the tide to roll in and set the *Diana* upright again, when Captain Cooper yelled.

"Dirty lizards, move! We sail with the tide! Get those lines, rig sails, clear this beach, dammit, before I skin the lot of you and use your bones for ballast!"

"Captain!" Abe, who was on the other side of the beach, helping with the ropes that kept the *Diana* on her side and secured, put his hands to his mouth and called back to Cooper. "What is it?"

"It's Blane! He'll not get away from us!"

Frowning, Abe shaded his eyes and looked out to sea.

Jill followed his gaze and saw a shape moving parallel to the shore, far in the distance. It might have been a ship—if it was, it was far enough out that it wouldn't see the *Diana* in her hidden cove. Jill wondered how Cooper could not only identify it as a ship, but as the *Heart's Revenge* specifically—then saw her, once again, holding up the broken rapier piece on its string. Not only did it point toward the distant object, it jumped and shook, pulling on the string in Cooper's hand as if trying to break free.

Abe was still frowning. He didn't like this quest, Jill suspected. While the captain was yelling at the crew to get the ship rigged, Abe turned to Jill, Henry, and several of the others close by.

"Make sure all the fresh food and water we gathered is aboard. Get as much as you can up before we go running. And somebody drag on that useless surgeon."

"And that's why Abe's the quartermaster," Henry murmured as Abe went to give orders to haul gear back on board the ship. The others chuckled in agreement.

Working together, passing casks, crates, and baskets forward to where Henry pulled them aboard using a rope and pulley, they loaded the ship while Captain Cooper drove the rest of the crew to setting her upright and arranging the rigging. It took an hour to get the cannons on board; Cooper told them to wait and stow them properly when the ship was under way. Every minute that passed grew more urgent.

Finally, they were ready to go, but in this inlet, no wind blew to fill the sails, and the tide didn't give enough current to push them back to sea. That was the price for wanting a spot that was sheltered from wind and weather. But the pirates had a solution for everything: they towed the *Diana*. A couple of the crew went out in one of the rowboats, carrying an anchor and line with them. Out in open water, they dropped the anchor—the end of the line was still on the *Diana*. Back on deck, the strongest sailors in the crew hauled on the line. Jenks called out orders in rhythm. "Heave! Heave!"

Slowly, the ship began to move.

Jill watched, amazed, sure they wouldn't be able to budge the *Diana* from where she rested, her bottom just touching the sand, the waves of the incoming tide lapping against her unmoving hull. But they did, towing her, dragging against the anchor snagged at the bottom of the inlet. Jill leaned over the bow to watch. When she looked to shore, the trees of the jungle were moving, sliding past, however slowly. The swath of water between ship and shore grew wider.

When they passed over the anchor, the crew hauled it up. By then the current had caught them and carried them out past the sheltering sandbar that formed the inlet. The captain shouted orders about raising topsails and setting yards, and crewmen climbed the masts and shrouds like nimble squirrels to release the crackling sound of unfurled canvas.

The wind caught the sails, and the ship lurched, rising and falling as she rode the first big waves of open ocean. The slap of water striking the hull sounded like thunder.

Jill leaned on the rail, face into the wind, feeling salt spray kiss her skin after it splashed against the hull. She could almost feel the *Diana* moving faster, cutting through the water more smoothly without all the gunk on the hull. And she found herself smiling, actually happy to see the island receding, blue waves rolling away in every direction, to hear canvas rippling and ropes creaking. Happy to be sailing again.

Captain Cooper continued shouting orders, and the crew continued scrambling. More sails unfurled, more rigging came into play, and the ship picked up speed, almost leaping over the waves.

"There she is! Ship ahoy!" Henry shouted from the lookout at the top of the mainmast. He pointed off to starboard. Jill looked to the horizon but didn't see anything. As she squinted against the sun, the scene all looked like water and haze.

More orders, more rushing, more lines pulled, knots tied, sails unfurled. Jill didn't know how fast they were moving, but she had to hang on to one of the ropes on the mast to keep from losing her balance. Even with the delay, they caught up to the other ship.

She saw it by the spray of water. Knowing where to look now, she could make out the shape of it, its hull and sails, like a tiny picture of a toy boat, except it was obviously moving, cutting through waves, ocean splashing around it.

"Hoist the colors! Man the cannons!"

This was different than when they'd overtaken the slave ship. Nobody cheered, nobody laughed. Nobody ran up to the gunwales to see what was happening, waving swords and pistols over their heads. This time, everyone was busy, serious, bent to their work, and if they stole a moment to look over the water, it was with a frown. The crew who weren't trimming sails, helping the ship fly to its target, pounded to the cannons. Jill heard a new sound; rattling as hatches flew open in the sides of the boat, creaks and slams as those eight sleeping monsters were awakened, unlashed from their places, and rolled forward, ready to be loaded, fired. The whole ship groaned like a waking leviathan.

The next time Jill looked out over the water, the other ship was definitely closer. She could see people moving around on its deck, specks of urgent motion.

From the *Diana*'s mainmast, the leering skull with the rose and sword crossed beneath it snapped and sang, a herald of doom.

Jill looked for Henry in all the chaos and saw him emerge from the aft hatch in the deck. He had an armful of weapons.

He caught her gaze across the deck. "How are you with a pistol?"

Jill shook her head. "I've never held a gun in my life."

The quirk of a smile returned to his lips, making him look a little crazy. He said, "Well then, you'll just have to keep hold of your sword and wait for the real fighting." He ran off on another chore, leaving her gaping.

"Wait a minute—sword fighting? We're not really going to . . . there's not really going to be—"

Well, she'd just about asked for it with all the practicing, hadn't she?

A boom of distant thunder made Jill flinch. Across the water, a cottony puff of black smoke burst from the side of the ship and floated. Then another, and another. More thunder followed.

We're all going to die, she thought, too numb to be scared.

9

ATTACK

Thirty or so feet out from the ship, columns of water sprayed upward, a row of giant splashes as a cannonball skipped over the water, impressive but harmless. The other ship's cannon fire had missed.

Captain Cooper shouted from the helm. "Ha! He's wasting his gunpowder on us, my mates. Let's show him how a real ship fights!"

Her crew shouted. Even the ship seemed to jump in echo of her words.

"Is it really Blane?" Jill saw the smudge of a black flag flying from the other ship's mast, but she couldn't see its details. She wanted to think she'd been mistaken about the broken rapier reacting so violently.

"Yeah—look at the flag, the shape of her, the set of her sails," Henry said. "And we wouldn't go after any other pirate folk like this."

The ship had a gunnery mate—Tennant. His voice hollered across the deck. "Powder! Ram!"

Then came a pause, as if everyone on board held their breath. Sea splashed and gulls cried, and both ships seemed poised on the water. They might have frozen that way forever, until everything happened at once.

Cooper called, "Stand by to fire!"

"Ready!" Tennant shouted.

"Let go the sheets! Go to larboard!" Sails flapped, and the ship turned, just a hair, leaning to the left as if she was going to turn away from the *Heart's Revenge*, until the *Diana's* starboard side faced her. Then the captain shouted, "Tennant, fire, damn you!"

Every cannon on that side fired. Jill buckled over, covering her ears. The whole ship vibrated, rattling, and didn't stop, as if the force of the guns would shake apart every timber. Shiver me timbers. . . .

The air filled with smoke and fire. She coughed at the reek of sulfur in her lungs, which only made her inhale more of the thick, ash-filled air. Some of the crew had tied scarves over their mouths. She still had her scarf from the beach, and she did the same.

Henry was laughing, but Jill couldn't hear the sound, only see his mouth open.

Leaning close to her he said, "There's your broadside!"

Everyone who wasn't tending guns or sails looked out to see what effect the round of cannon fire had had. Jill couldn't see, but then she wasn't sure what she was looking at. Smoke obscured both ships. The *Heart's Revenge* seemed to be bobbing in the water, as if it had stopped moving entirely. Its sails seemed loose, confused.

The captain yelled another set of orders, and the ship turned, looking to cross in front of the enemy ship. They sailed, running fast, like hunting down easy prey. Jill could start to make out individual lines among the other ship's rigging.

Cooper was shouting, Tennant was ordering the cannons to reload, Jenks was yelling at the crew to do incomprehensible things to the sails, and that still left a chunk of the crew—Abe among them—gathered by the side of the ship, muskets, pistols, and swords in hand, waiting. Unlike the encounter with the slave ship, they expected to bring the *Diana* alongside and fight.

Judging distance and speed on the open water was deceptive. The *Heart's Revenge* looked like she wasn't moving, but in fact she'd been swinging around, just like the *Diana* was. While the *Diana* was trying to get in front of the other ship, the other seemed to be turning, preventing her from doing so, keeping its own cannons pointed toward her.

All Jill could guess was that there'd be more cannon fire, more smoke, and more chaos.

"We're coming in too fast," Henry murmured.

Jill didn't have time to ask him to explain. Another roar of thunder sounded, another mass of smoke erupted from the *Heart's Revenge*. This time, the *Diana* was within range, and this time, the longest side of her enemy, and the most cannons, were facing them.

"Get down! Down!" Abe shouted, and everyone fell. Hit the deck, Jill thought, wondering if that was where the phrase came from. She curled up against the foremast, arms covering her head. Something exploded, and debris fell.

Another round of cannon fire burst from the other ship, which didn't make sense to Jill—she'd been paying attention to the *Diana*'s cannons; she knew how long they took to reload. Then she realized: The *Heart's Revenge* had only fired half its cannons in the first round. They fired the other half while reloading the first.

The *Diana* returned fire almost in the same moment, so that the whole ocean was nothing but thunder, shot whistling overhead, smoke, and the stink of gunpowder. How could anyone see in this? How could anyone even dare to lift their head to see what was going on and decide on the next move?

Or maybe it was like fencing, a duel of move and countermove, only between two ships instead of two people with swords. That she could understand. What she didn't get here were the moves. This was nothing like parry and riposte. This was about putting yourself in the right place to blow the crap out of the other person, without getting blown up yourself. There were no other defensive moves except to just not be there.

Captain Cooper was so determined to get at the *Heart's Revenge* that she'd put the ship in a position to get the crap blown out of it.

The ship heeled over in a sudden change of direction, causing the deck to slant at an unbelievably steep angle. Jill lost her place and rolled, convinced that the whole thing was going to tip over and dump them all in the water. But a wave caught it and set it to rights. No longer huddled by the side, Jill was able to look around.

Instead of dark, weathered wood, several places, including part of the mainmast, now showed pale splinters. It looked like some large animal had gnawed a piece from it and left shreds of splinters hanging out.

And still Cooper hollered at the crew not to back down,

not to waver, to keep the helm heaving over, steering them into the maw of those cannons. The *Diana* shuddered as her own cannons fired a volley in reply. Cannonballs screamed, slicing through the air.

Jill tried to be calm. She tried to imagine herself in a bout, in a quiet gymnasium during the finals of a tournament. There, she could always calm herself, center herself, focus outward, and do what needed to be done, let the skills she'd practiced until they were worn into her muscles come to the fore and guide her.

It didn't work. She was in the middle of a war of noise and stench.

The best and smartest thing she could do would be to find a place to hide, curl up there as small and out of the way as she could, and wait for it to end. But she didn't, because she couldn't think of any place on the ship that would be safe from the thunder, from the pounding of cannonballs that could rip through the thickest wood.

Then there was the screaming.

Members of the crew had fallen. Some of them picked themselves up; others didn't, but instead writhed and moaned, clutching their heads or arms. Blood spilled from them. Again, blood soaked into the nice clean deck she'd spent so much time scrubbing. Jenks had a gash on his face, but he didn't seem to notice; he kept going from mast to mast, shouting up at crewmen working the sails, trying to keep the ship moving.

In the middle of the deck, a young sailor named Saul tried to pick himself up, but he couldn't. Even through the smoke and the haze, Jill could see the bleeding wound in his arm and the splintered bone showing through skin. She didn't have a job, not in the middle of all this, and she didn't know what else to do, so she ran to him.

Stumbling to a crouch beside him, she grabbed his good arm and propped him up. "Don't move. Your arm's broken."

He looked at the wounded arm, maybe for the first time, then turned his gaze skyward, wincing. "Oh Jesus!"

"It's going to be okay, we can go someplace safe, below-decks." Away from where the cannons were roaring and the ship was splintering around them. Cannons rumbled on wooden wheels against the deck, sparks flew, the stench of sulfur choked away the good air, and Tennant's shouting echoed. The deck was roasting, heat radiating from the iron cannons. Many of the men who worked the cannons went shirtless, and their skin gleamed with sweat.

"I fell, fell off the yard. Stupid!" Saul said around gritted teeth.

She had thought of him as just another one of the crew, one of the rough and snarling pirates, barefoot, with worn clothes and a mocking attitude. Close to him, though, seeing his face tense and lined with pain, she saw that he was maybe even as young as her and Henry. They were all young.

Getting him belowdecks might not be the right thing to do, but she couldn't think of anything better, so she pulled his arm over her shoulder and urged him to his feet.

"You! Girl!" A new voice was shouting at her. She looked back, twisting to see over her shoulder, and there was Emory, the surgeon. Someone had untied him. He had his own injured man, Martin, his face covered with blood, propped up next to him. "Bring him here! Quickly!" He gestured down the steps.

She helped her injured man stumble over to follow Emory into the depths. They took the stairs carefully, Jill trying to balance both her charge and herself while barely being able to see. The lower deck was dark as a cave after the light and noise of the battle.

Emory led them around the steps into a relatively clear space along the prow. There were already two other men lying there, cradling limbs, covered in blood, moaning. A pair of lanterns hung from the beam overhead. They swung on their pegs, throwing dancing shadows over them all, making the scene even stranger.

"Put him down there," Emory said, depositing his own burden against a bulkhead. The surgeon looked at her and her injured sailor, and frowned. "God, what a mess. You, go back up and bring down anyone else."

There wasn't anything like a hospital here, not even a table or a basin of water. She didn't know what Emory could do to help them. With a sick feeling in her gut, she realized that maybe he couldn't do anything, and they were bringing the men here to die, out of everyone's way.

She ran back up and looked for the next injured crewman.

Cooper still yelled orders, commanding the ship to move, to give chase to the *Heart's Revenge*, which had now turned, managing to catch a wind that carried it away from the *Diana*. They'd unfurled sails, speeding their escape. Jill couldn't tell how badly they'd been damaged, if at all; the other ship seemed perfectly functional. On the other hand, the *Diana* wasn't responding to the captain's orders. It might have been because there wasn't enough crew standing to carry them out, but that didn't seem to be the case because there were certainly enough people running around the deck and shouting.

When Jill looked up to the canopy of ropes and sails that was the *Diana*'s engine, she saw death. Cut and burned lines swung free, useless. Sails drooped from broken yards, slumping across masts and rigging. One of the smaller sails—Jill tried to remember its name, one of the triangular sails tied off to the bowsprit—was still trimmed, spread and ready for action. But it wasn't enough to move them forward with any speed. It caught the air and sent them slowly downwind.

Captain Cooper leaned over the side, screaming at her adversary, no matter that he couldn't hear. "That's it, run like the scurvy worm you are, you couldn't board me and face me down like a real man because you're a worm! A craven worm! Dirt under my shoe, Blane, wretched dirt under my shoe!" And so on, with hardly a breath between curses.

The air began to clear, and Jill's legs turned soft, rubbery. She sat heavily on the deck, right where she was, under a shattered piece of mast and next to a smear of blood. Tipping her head back, she studied the changed landscape of the rigging. What had been smooth and arcing sail, taut rope, a functional pattern, was now chaos. The broken sails seemed tired, and the severed ropes swung back and forth, lazy and purposeless.

"Chain shot," Henry said. He slumped down beside her, his legs folding as bonelessly as hers had. She looked at him blankly. Nodding toward the wounded rigging, he explained, "They weren't trying to kill us dead. They weren't firing all cannonballs. They fired chain through the rigging to rip it all to pieces. So they could get away without us following them. Bloody curs."

"What now?" Jill said. She thought she knew the answer: Wasn't much else they could do but fix the sails and rigging, repair the ship, bandage the wounded, and continue on.

Henry shook his head. "Captain's taking this personal. The crew might have a say about that if she's not careful."

Captain Cooper had run out of curses, though it had taken her awhile. Now she leaned one hand on the side and watched the *Heart's Revenge* race away. The ship had receded back to the size of a toy bobbing on the horizon.

After the last hour, Jill was likely to approach any fight with Blane personally as well.

"Is it always like this? Every time you fight with another ship?"

His grin went crooked. "We hardly ever fight. That's the trick. This . . . this is something else. There's a war been brewing between the two captains. Since before my time here."

"It's not worth it. It can't be," she said. "Getting shot to pieces by cannonballs, spending the rest of the time waiting to be shot, dying here in a bleeding mess a million miles from anywhere."

"Everyone dies, see," Henry said. "I could do it here among friends, or on a merchant ship with a ruddy bastard for a captain getting whipped every day of my life. It's worth it to me."

She didn't agree. Slumping back, she blinked up into the limp sails.

"Hey there, you're hurt," Henry said, and touched her arm.

Jill flinched away reflexively, skittish. But she looked down and saw her arm for the first time. It was bleeding. She hadn't noticed it and couldn't remember how it had happened. A gash sliced across her left bicep, tearing off half the sleeve of her shirt and biting into the flesh underneath. The wound gaped open and poured blood down her arm. Something must have cut it open when she fell, or some piece of flying debris must have knocked into her. How could she not have felt it happen?

Stress, adrenaline, distraction. Even now, looking at the split skin, it didn't really hurt. But she suddenly wanted to faint as her stomach flipped over.

Henry pulled her arm back and started ripping off the sleeve.

"I don't know how that happened, I don't remember," she murmured.

He took the piece of sleeve, wrapped it around the wound, and jerked it tight. She winced and bit back a shriek.

A scream from belowdecks echoed what she was feeling. It sounded like torture, and it didn't stop.

"What's that?" Jill said, suddenly upright and aware.

Henry's mouth puckered, like he'd eaten something sour, and he wouldn't look at her. "I'd guess the surgeon's taking someone's arm or leg off."

"What?"

"Like as not someone broke an arm too badly to be set. Better to have it off," Henry said, speaking casually, as if it didn't matter, and staring at the open hatch.

Saul, whom she'd helped belowdecks—no, it couldn't be him. He wasn't hurt so badly. Was he? "But it was just broken, a broken arm can be fixed. It just needs to be set and bandaged."

"It can't be fixed," he argued. "You try to tie it up, it'll swell and get rotten. Then it'll kill him. Better this way."

Jill was standing now, a hand on her own bandaged arm, staring at the hatch, imagining the scene that was happening below. Maybe Henry was wrong, maybe the surgeon wasn't really amputating Saul's arm. Why would he? And without anesthetic, without drugs or hot water or antibiotics—it was a wonder these people weren't all dead.

She was lucky she wasn't dead. And what would happen to her if she stayed here much longer?

The screaming stopped, and after that terrible sound the ship seemed quiet. The sounds of people moving, calling to each other, pounding wood and throwing lines, seemed peaceful.

"Oy, Tadpole! You're bleeding."

Jill spun to find Abe coming toward her.

"Emory should have a look at you," the quartermaster said.

"No," Jill said. "No, it's fine, it's just fine." She covered the wound with her hand, but blood had already soaked through the bandage and was leaking down the arm. She couldn't hide it.

Emory appeared at the top of the steps then, emerging from below like a creature rising up from underwater. He was wiping bloody hands with a soiled cloth. A red film covered his arms nearly to the elbows, and his shirt was stained with great patches of scarlet.

"Who's next?" he said.

"Tadpole's cut her arm," Henry said.

"No, I'm okay, it's okay." Jill backed away.

"I'll just have a look at it." Emory gestured her forward.

"It's only a scratch, don't cut my arm off!"

The surgeon looked away, hiding a silent chuckle. "If it's not broken or rotten, I promise you I won't cut it off, and if you don't let me stitch it up, it'll grow rotten."

With Abe on one side of her and Emory on the other, she was fairly sure she wouldn't escape, but she didn't much like the idea of the surgeon stitching the wound. Her arm throbbed thinking of it. But she remembered the gaping flesh and knew she probably needed stitches. Her shoulders slumped, and she started picking off the bandage.

"I'll get my kit," Emory said.

Ten minutes later, she was sitting on the deck, trying not to watch while Emory stitched the wound with a needle that didn't seem sharp enough and thread that felt like it should have been used to mend sails. Henry had given her a mug of rum, and she'd drunk it. It didn't dull the pain, but it made her not care so much.

"This isn't so bad," Emory said. "You'll have a scar to tell stories about. Badge of honor."

She slouched sullenly, trying not to think about how he hadn't disinfected anything. She'd splash some of the rum on the wound later. And wouldn't that hurt like anything?

"You're glum," Emory said, by way of distraction.

"I hate this," she said.

"Well, what did you think was going to happen, signing articles on a ship like this?"

"I didn't plan on this, I'm not supposed to be here. They said they were going to throw me overboard if I didn't sign. What else was I supposed to do?"

"I'm sure you can explain it all to the judge before they hang you for piracy."

Jill pulled away to look at him.

He looked back. "You see, when this ship is taken by

the English, I'll explain to them that I was a prisoner, taken against my will when my ship was captured, and that I've nothing to do with any of these folks. They'll let me go. What will you do? How will you explain when they take the book and see your name written down? You'll hang with the rest of the dogs. Unless you help me."

His hard words belied the gentle way he tended her wound, holding the skin closed, making little stitches to seal it. She looked away again, unhappy at the way the blood and water dripped from his hands.

"We won't be captured. That's all," she said.

"Of course we won't," he said with false cheer and an insincere grin.

10

RECOVER

They had spent that week onshore in Jamaica cleaning and repairing the *Diana*, and now they had to do it all over again, at sea.

No one had died, which amazed Jill. For all the blood and wreckage, death seemed the obvious outcome. But she was relieved. That was a close enough brush with death for her. A dozen of the crew, including her, had been injured, three of them seriously enough that they stayed belowdecks, under Emory's watch. Two of those had splinters and shrapnel in their legs and torsos, had lost blood, and needed rest. Jenks had bandaged the cut on his forehead—the scrap of cloth was streaked with dried blood. Emory had amputated one arm, and Saul would need time to heal.

Jill almost felt like she'd doomed him by bringing him to Emory's attention. Surely the arm could have been set, surely such drastic treatment could have been avoided. No one else seemed to think so, and the amputation was treated as a matter of course. She kept thinking that it didn't have to happen—back home, it never would have happened.

All the other injuries were to the *Diana* herself, and the crew set about healing her. The supplies they'd stolen off the slave ship proved to be useful—they had fresh sail and rope to replace the destroyed rigging. Carpenters among the crew checked the masts and shored up the damaged areas, securing timbers to weakened parts, almost like splints.

Jill was set to scrubbing the decks again, clearing away splinters and debris, throwing buckets of scrap overboard. And getting rid of more blood. She'd seen more spilled blood in the last two weeks than in the whole rest of her life.

And still, Jill and Henry practiced swordplay. She'd felt helpless during the battle, and she didn't feel helpless with a sword in her hand. She never wanted to see another battle. But if she did—and if they were boarded next time—she wanted to be able to defend herself and not cower on deck while debris rained down around her.

Swordplay was different on the deck of a rocking ship

than it was on a sandy beach. Jill learned the trick of it quickly. You always wanted to keep your knees bent and loose when you fenced; it kept you nimble, able to respond and move, advancing and retreating quickly while keeping good balance. The less you worried about where your feet were the more you could focus on the blade—yours and your opponent's. On a rocking deck, she just had to keep even more loose and nimble, so that her legs moved under her to keep her balance while her upper body—and her sword—remained steady. Then Henry got tricky, jumping onto the shrouds, swinging from a line to the deck, fighting from the boom or even the gunwales, risking losing his balance to get her in a bad spot. Then he'd have the high ground, the position of strength—and they were fencing in three dimensions, not just the back-and-forth of competitive strip fencing. It was maddening—but thrilling. She could feel herself getting better. When she and Henry fought, everything else, all her problems, and the fact that she was so far from home, faded away.

All this time, Captain Cooper stayed at the helm, staring through her spyglass to open sea, or checking the direction of her makeshift compass. The rapier tip always pointed away, to where the *Heart's Revenge* had sailed.

In a moment of quiet, Jill crept toward the helm, expecting the captain would yell at her to get back to work, and

find some new chore for her. The captain glanced at her—
and didn't yell. Encouraged, Jill nodded at the rapier point,
resting in Cooper's hand.

She wanted to touch it—it was why she'd picked it out
of the sand in the first place, and kept it. It still seemed to
whisper secrets to her, just out of her hearing.

"How does it work?" Jill asked.

Cooper gazed over the water. "That's 'How does it work,
sir.'"

Jill glared. "Sir. How does it work? How does it know?"

"Blane's got the rest of the sword," she said. "That's
how."

"Can it do anything else?" Jill asked. Like reveal the
secret of how she got here, and how to get home.

Regarding the pitted steel, Cooper shrugged. "I don't
know. The sword it came from has power—that's why it
wants to get back. What do you think it can do?"

"I don't know. But I think it has something to do with me."

This time, Cooper looked at her, her eyes narrowed,
showing wrinkles from so much time squinting in the sun.
"You do, do you? What, then?"

If she could explain it, she wouldn't need to ask. "All I
know is I found it, then I fell into the water, and then all this
happened." Jill spread her arm to show the *Diana*, its crew,
and the ocean around them.

"And you think, somehow, this has the power to undo it all?"

"I don't want to undo it—" And Jill stopped, because she didn't want to forget this. She didn't want it to have never happened, even the worst parts, like the battle, the amputated arm, and the slave ship. She wanted to remember Nanny, the nighttime sky, and learning to fight with Henry. "But I want to go home. And if some kind of magic brought me here, then it can send me back."

Cooper might have yelled at her about being part of the crew and never going home; but she didn't. Instead, she looked sad, her expression turning soft. Jill hadn't expected that.

"Get back to work, Tadpole," Cooper said finally. Jill did so.

During the evening meal, Captain Cooper called for order and addressed the crew.

"Blane's headed east, that's all I know," she said, her voice carrying.

"It's what a bit of rotten steel told you," Jenks said, a thought echoed by noises of agreement. The soiled bandage over his eye made him seem even more surly.

"Aye, and we all have reason enough to curse the man and do what we can to keep him off these waters. He's never done a one of us any favors."

"None's arguing with you there, Captain. But we haven't taken a real prize in weeks. We signed on for the loot, not a bloody foxhunt."

"We take Blane, we take his loot," Cooper said.

"If he don't sink us first," another man said—John, one of Jenks's mates. More grumbling followed.

The captain went on. "Here's my notion: We sail to Nassau. Refit what we need, unload what we have to unload—drink us a bit of ale while we're there." Murmurs of agreement met this idea. "And we can also get word about Blane and where he's gone to, and what he's planning."

Jenks was still frowning when he stood and said, "I call for a vote."

"Where else do you suggest we go?" Cooper said.

"No. Not a vote on destination. I call a vote for captain," he said.

The ship was quiet for a moment, everyone falling still and looking at the first mate. His face was shadowed in the setting sun, making his glare and his scowl seem worse. He gripped his mug in both hands and ignored the wondering looks that turned to him. Jill thought he might have been drunk.

Jill leaned close to Henry to whisper, "What's happening?"

Quietly and urgently, he answered, "Jenks is tired of

chasing after Blane. He wants to replace Captain Cooper."

"With who?" she said.

Before Henry could answer, Captain Cooper gave a brash laugh, drawing their attention.

"What?" she said to Jenks. "And vote for yourself instead? Think you can do better, then?"

Jenks nodded. "Aye, you've forgotten what we're here for. For prizes, not revenge!"

Jill felt cold—she didn't want Jenks as captain. She thought of what would have happened to her that first day if Jenks had been in charge—and thought she'd have ended up back in the water, or worse.

"You think I'm afraid of a vote?" Cooper said. "You think I'll start sobbing like a wee maid? What about the rest of you? Are you with him or me?"

The crew was silent.

"A vote's been called," Abe said, his voice clear. He climbed into the shrouds, putting him above the gathering. "Are you sure, Jenks?"

"That fight today never should have happened. Of course I'm sure."

Some grumbles of agreement echoed him, and some of dissent. Surely this wouldn't end peacefully.

"Then we vote."

Jill gripped Henry's arm. "What happens now? What

happens if Cooper loses the vote?"

He shook his head, his jaw set, his brow furrowed with worry. "The captain and those loyal to her will be set ashore, and the *Diana* sails on."

"She won't lose, will she?" Jill said. Henry didn't answer.

Abe brought out two wooden buckets. Meanwhile, the crew passed out markers among themselves—they looked like buttons of metal and bone—then lined up in front of Abe. Jill hung back, but Henry pulled her in line.

Abe held up the bucket in his right hand, then his left. "This is a vote for Captain Cooper. This is a vote for First Mate Jenks. Captain?"

Cooper was first, and she held up her marker for all to see with a flourish and placed it in the right-hand bucket. Many of the crew cheered, which made Jill feel a little better. Cooper couldn't possibly lose. Jenks was next, and of course he put his marker in the left-hand bucket. More people cheered. Jill didn't like the way Henry was frowning.

Abe put his marker in Cooper's bucket.

One by one they cast their votes. Jill tried to keep track of how many people dropped buttons in Cooper's bucket, but the line moved quickly and she lost count. Far too many people put their markers in Jenks's bucket. The line stepped forward, and Jill was standing before Abe.

"Last vote, Tadpole," the quartermaster said. He pointed to the buckets. "Cooper or Jenks?"

She dropped her button for Captain Cooper.

"Henry, boy. Help me count," Abe said. The two hunched over the buckets and began counting.

The crew watched while Abe counted, slow and careful, putting each button in a pile by its bucket. Henry counted out the buttons a second time. Jenks paced, taking swigs from a bottle tucked in his hand. Cooper stood at the helm, waiting calmly.

"I'll have you fined for drunkenness, Jenks," Cooper said to him.

"Not if you're stuck by yourself on a godforsaken spit of land, you won't," he called back.

When Abe stood, everyone turned their attention to him.

"I have the count!" He waited for a dramatic pause. Jill was about to scream at him, but someone did it for her.

"Just tell us what it is, you black dog!"

Then Abe smiled. "Jenks has eighteen votes. Captain Cooper has twenty-seven and is our captain still."

A cheer went up—and most everyone cheered. Probably even a few who had voted for Jenks. No one questioned Abe or asked for a recount—he'd been voted quartermaster and everyone trusted him. They'd all watched him count. Jill might have expected fighting to break out, the whole rowdy crew taking sides and battling for control of the ship. But they respected the vote. Not even Jenks protested.

Cooper stepped slowly across the deck to where Jenks stood, his bottle of rum hanging at his side.

"Jenks, you're the best sailing master on the seas. But I can't let this pass."

Jenks took a long draw on the bottle, then coughed. His look turned sad. "I'm only tired, Captain. I meant no harm."

"And what happens the next time you're angry and drunk and you call me out again?"

"I won't, I promise—"

"I don't believe you. Abe, Tennant, get one of the boats ready."

"No, Captain, I didn't mean anything!"

Jill found Henry again. "Now what's happening?"

"He brought it on himself," he said.

Abe, Tennant, and half a dozen others hurried around the rowboat, arranging the pulleys that would lower it into the water, and loading it with a bucket of water, a bag of food, and an oar.

Then they loaded Jenks into the rowboat. You didn't need an island to maroon someone.

As the boat was lowered toward the water, Cooper

stood at the side, holding a pistol aimed at Jenks. The first mate—or former first mate—had turned sullen, splayed on the bottom of the boat, glaring up at the captain, unable to rebel any further.

The captain called to the rest of the crew, "Anyone else rather put their lot in with Jenks than with me, if you think I'm such an awful captain?"

They were all leaning on the side with her, watching, silent. Not even Jenks's supporters made a sound. Cooper made sure to look at each of them, hold their gazes, and stare right through them. Every one of them ducked away. The ropes and pulleys creaked as the rowboat sank to the water.

When the boat finally touched down to be rocked and shaken by waves, Jenks shouted, "Curse you! Curse you all!" By then the boat had been cut loose to drift away as the wind pushed the *Diana* onward. His voice was quickly lost amid more common shipboard noises.

"Now," Cooper said, slipping the nose of the pistol under her belt. "We sail for Nassau. Then we go hunting like we ought to. We have a reputation to maintain. Any more arguments?"

None. The crew got to work as though nothing had happened. Jill looked back and saw a dark, foreign shape bobbing on distant waves. Then she didn't see anything.

Cooper never once glanced back.

Then the usual drinking started. By morning the *Diana* was repaired, the sails were unfurled, and the course set for the Bahamas.

Back where Jill started.

11

COUPÉ

Jill was learning to always notice the wind, where it was blowing and at what strength, and how it played against the sails. You didn't want the wind directly behind the ship—most of the sails' surface would be blocked by each other and the rest of the rigging. But if the ship was at a slight angle to the wind, the yards slightly turned, then every single sail would catch the wind's full strength and the ship would fly. And while you didn't want to be moving directly against the wind, a ship could still move into the wind by tacking, traveling at angles like following switchbacks up a steep hill.

Between islands, she couldn't have said where they were, and she could only vaguely guess their direction by the sun. The ship must have had a compass, a real one, and Captain Cooper must have had a map of some kind, or maybe she'd just memorized the location of every port and spit of land in the Caribbean. People were supposed to be able to navigate by the stars, but Jill hadn't learned the trick of it reliably yet. At night before going to bed, she'd lie on the deck, looking up into the sky, a vast, dark expanse filled with stars, packed with them like sprays of glitter. She'd never seen so many—there were almost too many to pick out individual stars. But somehow, Cooper knew where they were going, and one morning, a few days after the battle with the *Heart's Revenge*, the lookout high up on the mainmast called "Land, ho!" This time when Jill looked, she recognized the smear of shadow on the horizon that meant land.

The work began to trim the sails to take the *Diana* into port. Jill worked with the crew, pulling lines taut and tying off sails, until the ship rode the waves along New Providence Island and into Nassau's harbor.

This wasn't the Bahamas she remembered. When she came here with her family, Nassau was a postcard-perfect resort town. Rows of houses painted in bright colors had everything from shops to restaurants to government buildings. Crowds of tourists wandered on foot or took the little horse-drawn carts that lined up by the pier. At any given time a dozen huge cruise ships were docked on a long concrete jetty. A few miles away, a massive hotel dominated an inlet called Paradise Island. The only sign that the island had ever had anything to do with pirates or old sailing ships were the two crumbling forts looking out over the sea.

This was nothing like it.

She recognized the shape of the land, the long shore and sheltered inlet, the curved spit that would someday become Paradise Island, the hill that someone would look at someday and decide it would make a good fort, and the crowd of trees and vegetation, of which only a tamed remnant remained in the modern world. The forts had vanished—they hadn't even been built yet.

A dozen ships anchored along the harbor, a forest of masts. There was no large pier yet, so the ships staked out their own area of clear water and their crews rowed small boats to shore, where a narrow wooden pier provided access. A settlement covered a clear section of land. There were streets, buildings, wooden structures that seemed solid enough, with roofs, porches, doors, and windows. Smoke from a dozen cooking fires rose up. The tropical sun blazed down on the scene.

People moved through it all. She could see figures on most of the ships, and the shore was packed with people, workers loading and unloading stacks of barrels and boxes from ships, streets packed with carts and pedestrians. It was almost a traffic jam.

All those people looked just like the crew of the *Diana*: loose shirts and trousers, beards, unkempt hair, rowdy dispositions. They couldn't all be pirates, could they? But like nearly everything else she'd encountered since falling off the tour boat, the place seemed dangerous—even deadly. Still, she had to go ashore. This was where she'd started, where she'd found the rapier shard.

"Any navy friends?" Cooper asked.

"No," Abe said, studying the ships and shore through the spyglass. "Clear as can be."

"Any sign of the *Heart's Revenge?*"

"Not a hint of her," Abe said.

Cooper shaded her eyes and nodded out to a vessel at the far end of the harbor. "God, is that Rackham's ship?"

"I believe it is," he answered.

"Bloody hell," she said. "Wonder who else is about?"

Jill wondered who Rackham was.

"Ready to drop anchor, mates!"

The crew came to new life, simmering with smiles and laughter, excitement about the chance to go onshore, to see faces other than the ones on the ship, to eat fresh food and drink clean—or at least cleaner—water. They were all so at home here, when Jill kept seeing threats.

She was standing at the prow, watching the crew drop anchor when Henry came up to her, the rapier she'd been using to practice in hand, along with a belt and hanger.

"Nassau's rough. You'll need a weapon if you're going ashore," he said.

"Am I going ashore?"

"Why not? You're crew. But you only get to wear it if you can walk like you know how to use it. Otherwise folk'll treat you like a target. Think you can do that?"

She took the rapier and belt. "What do you think?"

"Right, then." He seemed pleased.

They tendered ashore using two rowboats. Just enough of the crew, a half a dozen, stayed aboard to "keep anyone from thinking they could steal her, but not so many that they'd want to steal her themselves," Henry said with his usual smile. Everyone else seemed all too happy at a chance to see civilization again. If historic Nassau could be called civilization. Jill wasn't too sure about that.

A wooden pier extended from the shore; smaller boats could tie up here. Rowboats, longboats, fishing boats with long oars and single masts. The waves lapped against dozens of hulls, and noises from the shore carried over the water. Donkeys and horses whinnying, goats bleating, chickens in crates clucking as they waited to be carried aboard ships heading out. Dockmen with rough leather shoes and caps, loose trousers and shirts, much like the pirates themselves, worked carrying wooden boxes and barrels, the cargo that had become so familiar. Everyone, from drovers on the street to fishermen in their boats, paused to take in the newcomers, Captain Cooper with her belted coat and her rowdy crew of pirates. Jill could almost see the rumor traveling from the docks through the streets to the town. The attention made her want to hide; but if she had to be here at all, she was grateful to be part of a group that seemed to inspire awe. Maybe people would leave her alone.

"Stand up straight, Tadpole," the captain said over her shoulder at Jill.

Jill had been slouching, skulking, really, under all those gazes. Glaring at the captain, she rolled her shoulders back and tried to look cocky, like the rest of them.

Saul accompanied them to shore. The stump of his missing left arm was swaddled with a thick bandage, giving no clue as to what the wound looked like underneath. His face was pursed, knotted with pain. Every few minutes he took a swig from a flask, no doubt filled with rum. He stood tall and looked straight ahead, glaring almost, daring anyone to feel sorry for him. On the dock, Captain Cooper handed him a bag of coins—it was part of the articles, bounty for a lost limb. He took it, awkwardly holding the flask under his good arm while he shuffled the pouch of coins from hand to pocket. The captain squeezed his shoulder, said a few words, and the injured man nodded curtly.

Then he left the crew for good, walking off into town alone.

"Stay sharp, keep your ears to the ground. When it's time to leave it'll be in a hurry, so you'd best keep close," Captain Cooper told the crew. With that, most of them scattered, moving off in small groups.

"You're with me, Tadpole," Cooper said to her, and Jill blinked at her, startled. Cooper took the broken piece of rapier from her pouch, let it dangle, and checked its direction: east, it settled. "He could be anywhere," she muttered.

"Where are we going?"

"We're going to track down the gossip on Blane."

A group of them went into town together: Captain Cooper, Abe, a couple men of the crew, Henry, and Jill. The streets were packed mud, rough and rutted. They kept to the side to avoid the carts and horses that traveled back and forth, wagons hauling crates, or travelers on some mission. Henry explained there were settlements up and down the coast, plantations that a few hearty souls tried to keep working—despite the fact that the pirates had been running the island for years now, since the British governor had packed up and left. Now the island was essentially lawless.

The pirates liked it that way just fine—they could bring their stolen cargos here and sell them to merchant ships with captains who didn't much care where the goods had come from, only that they were cheap. Industry to support the pirate trade had also moved in—carpenters and shipwrights; suppliers of food, ammunition, rope, and sails; and taverns, just waiting to cater to crews who had been at sea for weeks. Lots of taverns.

Cooper took them to one of these. They'd walked for ten or fifteen minutes from the docks, along the wider main street, then turned a corner to a narrow lane, then to an unpainted, sprawling house tucked into the first edges of wilderness—leafy shrubs, woody underbrush, stretches of grass and sand. A sign hanging above the door showed a painted ship and sea; it was the only clue that this wasn't just a house. Henry was grinning like he knew the place and was happy to be here, but Cooper seemed grim. She led them through an open doorway.

They walked inside and it was like the sun shut off. The windows were blocked by drapes or shutters. The haze of tobacco smoke added to the sense of claustrophobia. For a moment, Jill couldn't see anything. Slowly, her eyes adjusted, painfully blinking into sight.

The room was packed with pirates. She could tell without asking, just by the way they held themselves, the way they looked back at her, like they were sizing her up, judging her worth. And by the sly curves to their lips, the smiles that said they didn't care about a damned thing in the world. She'd lived with pirates for weeks now, and she recognized that look. It was Henry on that first day, hefting a rapier and looking right through her. She understood what he meant now about only carrying the sword if she could carry the attitude along with it. These people had to believe she could use it or they'd never stop picking on her.

When the pirates saw Captain Cooper, they shifted and murmured. A few looked away, as if hoping to avoid drawing her attention. But the ones who met her gaze straight on, who drew themselves up, seeming to offer a challenge— Jill paid attention to them.

Mostly, though, she hid behind Cooper and hoped she blended in as just another part of her crew.

"It's a bloody reunion. Everyone's here," the captain muttered to Abe.

"Then we should learn something of Blane," he replied.

"Everyone?" Jill asked Henry. "Everyone who?"

He was studying the crowd as well, and without his usual cocky confidence. He was trying to cover it up, but he seemed wary. "If the Royal Navy surrounded this place right now and burned it to the ground, there'd be no more piracy in the Atlantic and whatever captain was in charge could buy a title with the reward money. *Everyone's* here. Look."

He pulled her into a sheltered corner behind the bar that ran most of the length of one wall. The spot kept them out of the way but gave them a view of the room. Head bent close to her, he explained.

"There's Bellamy of the *Whydah*, and Stede Bonnet, who's really just a crazy old man but he's got a ship, so there you go. Charles Vane. Martel and Kennedy. Names to strike fear in the heart of any honest merchantman, though there's no such thing as an honest merchantman, as we say around here." He winked at her, like he expected her to laugh at the joke. Continuing, he nodded to a man sitting in the far corner. She'd noticed him already, a huge man, broad through the chest; he couldn't help but draw attention to himself. He wore a three-cornered hat over an immense nest of hair, long, black, flowing over his shoulders and continuing over his cheeks, jaw, and chin, covering his mouth. The thick beard grew halfway down his chest, and the man had knotted ribbons in it. He smoked a pipe with a long stem and gazed quietly over the crowd with dark, shining eyes.

"That there's Edward Teach. Even you've heard of him I expect."

"Blackbeard," she said, and couldn't help being in awe. "He's Blackbeard."

"Aye, he is. And may you never cross his path in battle."

She would just as soon never cross his path at all.

"And over there, the ones the captain's speaking to." They could see through a wide doorway into another part of the building, a room where a boisterous party was in progress. Captain Cooper stood over a trio in the corner. A man sat in a chair, mug in one hand and pipe in the other; he was outrageously dressed in a brightly colored jacket and flowered trousers. The two with him were women—at least Jill thought they were, though they dressed as men, in jackets and trousers, hats on their heads and hair bound up. One of them sat in a chair next to the man, arms crossed, glaring. The other stood behind them both, back to the wall and hand resting on the butt of a pistol tucked into her belt.

"That's Calico Jack Rackham," Henry said. "And the two pirate queens, Anne Bonny and Mary Read. As fierce a pair of witches who ever sailed. But not as fierce as our Captain Cooper, are they?"

"Are there many women pirates?" Jill asked.

"Hard to say. There's plenty who don't want to be found out, like Bessie and Jane, and no one hears about them. Only a few put themselves forward like them and Captain Cooper."

Jill thought they were powerful and frightening all at once. Anne Bonny, seated, had dark red hair that caught the light. And she studied Marjory Cooper closely as the captain spoke, as though if Cooper said the least thing wrong Bonny would spring from her chair, sword drawn, and run her through. But only if Read didn't get there first with her pistol. Read had dark hair and was more stout, more physical than Bonny. Bonny would use tricks in a fight; Read would just pound you.

Cooper, of course, didn't seem intimidated by either of them.

Mary Read looked over and caught Jill staring at her. Jill almost fell over; fear more than anything kept her rooted in place, staring back, wondering what she'd done to draw the pirate's attention, scrambling to figure out what she had to do to get away from it.

Then Read looked away, turning a smile as if chuckling to herself, and the spell was broken. Jill could breathe again.

Henry nudged her and put a mug in her hand.

"No, no more rum," she said, groaning. She was tired of rum. She wanted a nice cold Coke more than anything right now.

"It's not rum," he said.

She tasted it, an amber liquid, bitter and frothy. Definitely not rum. No—this was beer. It still wasn't a Coke, and it wasn't cold, but she sipped it anyway.

Jill imagined that this was where the pirates made deals.

For all the talking, laughing, and drinking going on, for all that the gathering seemed on the edge of turning rowdy, it never did. People sat close, chairs pulled together, bent over tables, talking. Maybe forming plans to raid together, maybe selling stolen cargo, maybe trading information about where their enemies had last been spotted, which ports to avoid and which were clear.

When she thought of those dozens of ships in the harbor, all with cannons, she understood why the navy didn't come along to capture everyone.

Abe had left the captain talking with Rackham and the others. He passed through the room, greeting and shaking hands with people who seemed happy to see him.

"What are they doing?" Jill asked Henry. "Why are we even here?"

"To find out what anyone knows about Blane. Without seeming like we are."

Moments later, Captain Cooper left the side room and returned to the main bar; Abe spotted her movement and joined her. The captain was full of business.

"Rackham's drunker than anything as usual, but Bonny says Blane's on the island. Doesn't know just where, of course. He raced ahead, got here before us. I count it as a stroke of luck. We'll have to bribe everyone here not to run to the old steer and tell him we're looking for him."

"Already done, Captain," Abe said, grinning.

"God, what a lot of rogues and thieves." She shook her head, but her lips curled in a smile, as if she could think of nothing better than rogues and thieves. "Let's go, all of you."

"But I've not finished my mug," Henry complained.

"Then drink fast," said the captain. And Henry did, upending the mug and draining it all.

Jill just set her drink aside and followed the captain and company outside, wincing in the sudden bright sun. It was like stepping from one world to another, a dark world of conspiracy into one of light and sea air.

"Tadpole?" the captain said, with only a cursory look over her shoulder to make sure Jill was really there.

"Aye?" Jill said reflexively, before she'd realized she'd said it. The reply had become habit.

"I need to you to stay on the ship for the rest of our time here."

"But—no, I can't—"

"You'll stay on the ship. Blane knows about that bit of rapier, Bonny says, like he can smell it on the air, and he may know about you as well. But he'll not have either one of you. So you'll stay on the ship."

She didn't want to stay on that ship a second longer. She had to find a way home, and the way home had to be here.

Maybe if she went back to the stretch of beach where she'd picked up that stupid piece of sword in the first place. She couldn't find a way home if she was on the ship.

Henry looked at her with interest, waiting for the next volley in the argument, but Jill didn't have one. She was too angry to speak. Cooper kept insisting she was part of the crew, but really the captain only saw her as a way to get to Blane. A pawn in a rivalry that had nothing to do with her. Not even worth being crew.

But she wasn't part of the crew. That was what Jill kept saying, that she wanted to get home, that she wasn't one of them. She shouldn't care what Cooper thought.

But she did, she discovered.

Jill marched along, feet pounding on the packed dirt road, not saying a word, biding her time. Making a plan.

12

BEAT

Captain Cooper sent Jill and Henry with a couple others of the crew to help row back to the *Diana*. The returning crew relieved the crew on watch, who took the rowboat back to shore, leaving Jill stuck on the ship.

Night had fallen, but the town of Nassau was still alive, lit by lanterns and torches, a glowing golden pool nestled by the harbor. Shouts, laughter, and songs from the taverns carried over the water, drunken pirates and merchant crews wandered the streets. A dog barked.

"What's she going to do when she finds Blane?" Jill asked Henry.

Henry sat on the bowsprit, leaning back, legs dangling high over the water. Jill sat near him on the gunwale, looking over the town. Her hand tapped nervously.

"I'm not sure," he said. "Run him through, I expect. She truly hates him."

"Why? Because he marooned her?"

"Some folk say it's because he broke her heart. They were once in love and he left her. In her fury she turned pirate and now roams the waves, vowing revenge." He took on the exaggerated tones of a storyteller.

"That's kind of melodramatic, isn't it?"

"It does seem a bit common for the likes of them, doesn't it? I'd guess it's something plain. He stole the ship from her, and she holds the grudge because that's how she is."

Whatever Cooper planned to do to Blane, the captain didn't much care what happened to Jill in the meantime. She stuck her on the ship to keep her out of the way. Jill frowned at the thought.

"What's wrong?" Henry asked, shifting to see her face, turned slightly away from him.

She shrugged and changed the subject. "You didn't have to stay here with me. I know everyone else is onshore, partying. You should have gone with them."

"Naw, this is fine. Besides, Captain ordered me to keep an eye on you."

Of course Henry hadn't stayed behind just to keep her company. Of course this was about Blane, again. Looking away, she muttered. "Or to keep me from escaping?"

He laughed. "And why would you do that?"

"I want to go home," she said, sighing.

"Do you even know where home is? We fished you out of the water, you didn't remember a thing."

That was the story they told themselves about her, because she hadn't told them the unbelievable truth. But Blane—maybe he'd know. If his broken sword brought her here, then maybe he'd know how to send her back.

Henry seemed inclined to sit on the prow talking all night— keeping an eye on her—but Jill said she was tired and needed sleep. She went below, curled up in her hammock, and waited. Nervous, she didn't worry about accidentally falling asleep. She had to wait until the ship was quiet, until she heard snoring from the handful of crew who remained aboard.

Someone would be keeping watch. One wrong step or stray noise would wake everyone. Very carefully then, very quietly, she climbed out of the hammock. Setting a bare foot on the wooden deck, then the other, she slipped to her feet, holding on to the hammock to keep it from swinging. They all went barefoot on board or on the beach, but she'd been given a pair of leather shoes to protect her feet on the dirt roads in town, and she put these on.

Sticking to the wall, she crept to the stairs, moving slowly to keep the floorboards from creaking. She checked one more time, but the two other people asleep in hammocks hadn't stirred. Climbing without a sound, she waited at the edge of the hatch and looked out. A few more men, including Henry, stood watch on deck. Rather, they drank rum and sang songs, picking up the scatterings of tunes carrying over the water from the town. They were drunk. She could probably walk right past them and they wouldn't notice.

Still, she remained careful and quiet.

They were on the starboard side of the ship, near the middle; so she crept to the port side, toward the bow, where the anchor was. Staying low, she kept to the shadows, easy to do in the sparse and scattered lantern light.

Using the anchor line, she climbed off the ship and into the water. The rope was thick and covered with slime; she had to practically hug it to make her way down, gritting her teeth and trying not to breathe too much. Then she swam, hoping there weren't sharks.

She brought the rapier with her, though she hated getting it wet. But she didn't dare go ashore unarmed. As long as she dried it off quickly, the water wouldn't hurt it. But the length of steel weighed her down and made swimming more difficult. Especially since she was trying to be quiet. She dog-paddled, keeping her head above water, and tried not to splash.

She avoided the pier, since people would be watching there, and swam to the beach instead. Once onshore, at the edge of Nassau proper, she only had to worry about running into anyone from the *Diana*. Especially Captain Cooper.

She hid behind a stack of crates waiting to be loaded onto a merchant ship in the morning. A scrap of canvas she found wasn't much good for drying anything off, but she was able to scrape most of the water off her rapier. The rest of her had to wait for the cool breeze coming in off the water. She started shivering; the sooner she got moving, the sooner she'd get warm. She couldn't worry about the cold.

The real trouble was, she only had one idea about where to start looking for Edmund Blane, and that was back at the pirate tavern.

She tied her hair up with a scarf and stuck a soft cap over it. The rest of her clothing was plain, nondescript: the loose shirt and trousers that everyone working on a crew at sea seemed to wear. She didn't think she could really pass as a boy. But she could hope that maybe people wouldn't look too closely at her. Maybe no one from the tavern that afternoon would recognize her as the girl who was with Captain Cooper.

The town wasn't large, the streets weren't complicated, so she found her way back to the alley and the sprawling house with its painted sign. Instead of going in, though, she slipped into the shadow of a nearby building, crouching at its corner and watching for Cooper and her crew. Some of them were surely here, but she wanted information and was willing to take the risk. The tavern seemed even more loud and boisterous—she could hear shouting and singing from the street. Those people who'd spent all day drinking were still at it. The settings had reversed: This time, the outdoors were dark, lit only with sparse lanterns, while the inside blazed with light.

Jill crept around the building, looking for a back entrance, to avoid drawing too much attention. She discovered the back door by the smell of the latrine. The rough, square shed stood only a few yards away from the house, nestled among the trees, and reeked about as sourly as she'd have expected a latrine outside of a bar where people had been drinking all day to smell. After she'd been watching a moment, a man stumbled from the shed, to the back of the tavern, and through the door.

She sneaked to the doorway and ducked inside.

For a moment, she lingered at the door, searching the room for anyone she recognized, for any reason to duck back outside and flee. No one seemed to notice her, which was good. This time, there wasn't just singing in the tavern, there was music played on fiddles and pipes, even dancing. And lots more women than she'd seen before, and with their bright dresses, low-cut bodices, curled hair, and made-up faces, it was pretty clear that they were working. Yet another reason for shore leave. Jill just wanted to stay out of the way.

Staying against the wall as much as she could with all the tables and chairs taking up spaces, and people using the walls to prop themselves up when they were on the edge of passing out, she moved through the first room and into the next, searching for someone who looked like they might be Edmund Blane. She imagined a towering villain with a scraggly beard and glaring eyes. And a broken sword at his hip. It was a haphazard way to search. But it was a start.

Then she saw someone she recognized, a woman sitting in the corner, smiling wryly, like she was also trying to keep out of the way but still enjoying the view. Mary Read.

Jill took a deep breath and approached. If she was too chicken to talk to the pirate, she should never have come here.

Read spotted her before Jill was ready to be spotted. She'd hoped to sneak up on her, come obliquely along the wall, maybe clear her throat to startle her, or tap her shoulder—though that might have gotten her punched, in hindsight. Instead,

Read looked over, as if she spotted Jill from the corner of her eye. As if she'd been waiting.

"Hey now, what have we got here?" Read announced, drawing the attention of the ragged, drunken bunch of pirates around her. Jill glanced at them, daring them to laugh at her, which they did. She glared.

"You're Marjory's new little pet, ain't you?" Read said. Her accent was thick, some brand of English Jill couldn't identify. "Has she sent you on some errand then?"

"No," Jill said. "She doesn't know I'm here."

Read raised a brow, as if surprised—maybe even impressed. Jill could hope. Read waved to a man, who handed over his mug of beer, and she passed it to Jill. Jill didn't want to drink; she didn't want to get muzzy headed. But she took it to be polite.

Here it went, then.

"I'm looking for Edmund Blane," she said.

"You and everyone else," Read said, looking away, taking a drink.

"I want to meet him."

"Why would you want to do that? Do you know what he's like?"

"No, not really. Just that Captain Cooper hates him. But he may be the only one who can help me."

"And why do you need help? Other than the fact that

you're a wee lass who's fallen in with pirates. And how did that happen?"

It would take too long to explain, and Read wouldn't believe her anyway, so Jill just shook her head.

"Ah yes, that's what I thought. Too complicated, it always is. Which ought to make it simple but it doesn't."

"How did you fall in with pirates?" Jill asked, wary, ready to run if the question made Read angry and she drew the short, stout cutlass at her belt, or one of the three pistols slung in a brace across her chest. Not that Jill was getting paranoid.

Read smiled into her beer. "It starts with putting on breeches and cutting your hair. Then you run away and join the army in secret. Then you think maybe you'll try a normal life—get married, find a respectable trade. And then your husband dies on you, so you go back to what you know best. You sign on to a ship and get captured by pirates and decide you like that best of all. Pirates are more forgiving than fathers, ain't they?"

Not her father, Jill thought with a pang, sure that he thought that she'd drowned long ago. Her parents and siblings surely thought her long gone. And there were all those times she'd been so wrapped up in the rest of her life she'd barely paid attention to them. She shouldn't have argued about going to the beach.

Jill couldn't tell if Read was drunk or not. She smelled of beer, but that may have been the rest of the room. The pirate studied her surroundings with a wary gaze, ready for action in a moment.

"But look at you," Read said. "You can't be all that green. You've seen action, eh?" She pointed to the bandage, still damp and stained from her swim, wrapped around Jill's bicep.

"It's just a cut."

"A battle scar's good enough to get you respect in this crowd," Read said. "Ah, but lose a leg, that'll really put folks in awe of you."

"I'd rather not."

Read chuckled.

Jill looked around, she hoped without seeming like she was, which probably didn't help at all with the attitude that she was supposed to be projecting. She tried to follow Henry's advice, to carry herself like she deserved to hold a rapier, but she was afraid she only appeared awkward.

Some of the crowd she recognized from the afternoon, which meant they'd been here most of the day. There were new faces as well. It was hard to keep them all straight.

"Where are your friends?" Jill asked Read.

"Who, Jack and Anne? Don't tell me I have to explain *that* to you?" Read said.

"Ah. No," Jill said quickly.

"You didn't actually think you'd find Blane here, did you?" Read asked.

"No," Jill said, frowning. "But I don't know where else to start looking for him."

Read leaned close, and the conversation turned hushed. "You really want to see Edmund Blane? You know what you're doing?"

"Yes, I do," Jill said, earnest, bluffing. She wasn't sure Read really believed her.

"I'll tell you what we told Marjory. Blane's up to something. Well, he's always up to something, but this is more than usual. He's not like the rest of us. Most of us who go on the account do it 'cause we're sick of taking orders from wicked captains who get rich off our labor. Out here, we have our code and our articles because that's what's fair. We're not so lawless, we have some honor, and most of all that means treating each other right. Blane's different, and if you want dealings with him you should know that. That rotten dog would be the king of all pirates if he could. Turn the Caribbean into his own empire. He ain't out here to live his life, he's in it for power."

And Jill knew: the power of a sword that called out to a broken piece of itself across the whole ocean. That drove Captain Cooper to such a rage.

"That's why Captain Cooper hates him so much?"

"For her it's personal," Read said.

"Why doesn't anyone else stop him?"

"Because a lot of men think like Blane, and they'll join up with him, happy for just a scrap of the power he promises. He's building an army that way. That lots of men are willing to sell themselves for a scrap of power is why the world's in the state it's in, isn't it?"

"Where can I find him?" Jill said

"Let me ask you something first. Cooper says you had a piece of his old rapier—how did you get it?"

"I told her—I just found it. Washed up in the sand."

Read studied her in earnest, as if trying to decide if she was lying. Jill glared, because she could tell the truth all she wanted, but what good did it do if no one believed her?

"He'll be wanting it back," the pirate said. "If he thinks you have it, he'll come looking for you."

"Maybe I should find him first then, right?" That was always a good fencing strategy—take the offensive.

"He's got a camp," Read said, lowering her voice even more. "Somewhere on the coast, no one really knows where. He doesn't even come into town for supplies. But walk straight east of here until you find the shore again. Then go south. But chances are you won't find anything at all."

"Thank you," Jill said, though when Read scowled she wished she hadn't.

"If I see Marjory, I'm telling her where you've gone."

Jill turned and slipped out of the tavern quickly. Heads turned, following her progress. So much for being secretive.

Outside, away from the lights and noise, she looked into the trees behind the tavern, and up at the sky. She may not have had the stars worked out after spending weeks on a sailing ship at sea, but she could judge direction by the position of the waning moon overhead. She knew which way east was, and started heading that way.

She held her rapier close to her leg to keep it from knocking and getting tangled up in vegetation. Progress was slow—without a path, she had to pick her way around tangled shrubs and crawling vines.

She couldn't get lost, she told herself. This was an island—if she walked long enough she'd simply reach ocean again. But she felt like she was walking far too long, past when she should have reached Blane's camp. Read hadn't said how far away it was.

All this assumed she continued walking in a straight line. She couldn't navigate by the moon and stars anymore—the sky was hidden by the tall, reaching canopy of the forest. After what felt like an hour of thinking the trees all looked the same, she wondered. She studied a grove where three trunks grew close together, surrounded by a dense thicket, tiny white flowers growing over it on vines. When she set off again, she made sure to walk in a straight line—how hard could it be? She fenced, which meant training on straight lines, fighting on straight lines. If nothing else, she knew how to walk in a straight line.

Except there was the grove again, and she was sure now it was the third or fourth time she'd seen it, the trees, thicket, and flowers together.

Nothing seemed fantastic to her anymore, and a horrible idea occurred to her. She'd stepped out of one strange time loop, the one that had brought her to the historical Bahamas and the land of pirates, and into another—a loop of endless wandering in this cool nighttime forest.

Instead of continuing forward this time, she turned around and started walking back the way she'd come—the way she thought she'd come. She could get back to Nassau, back to the pirate tavern, ask Mary Read what she'd done wrong or find someone who could really help her and not lead her astray. If anyone in this world could really help her, and that was the trouble, wasn't it? How did you trust a pack of pirates? Henry wasn't around to ask—and he'd always been happy to answer her questions. She missed having someone to trust. And yes, she realized. She trusted him. Maybe she should have asked him to come along.

She walked faster, determined to get out of the trap.

However focused she was on the way ahead, she saw it when a man stepped out of the undergrowth to her left. He loomed forward, arms outstretched as he lunged for her, and she skittered away, putting her hand on the hilt of her sword.

A pair of men appeared behind her, another pair in front of her, and she was surrounded. They leered at her as if this was a game, as if she was an animal they had hunted down and cornered, and now the real fun began. She could try to dart away, try to run and duck out of their reach, but they had placed themselves with just enough space for her to think she could escape. To encourage her to escape so they could have the pleasure of capturing her. It was a feint to try to draw her into a stupid move, like she'd done in fencing a hundred times. She didn't fall for it, but kept her place, circling, trying to keep the half dozen of them in view at the same time. She was too tense to be frightened, too ready to fight her way out. Time enough to be scared later.

Then they looked away from her, and that made her even more nervous, because they'd turned their attention to a new figure who'd stopped outside their circle.

This man was tall. He carried a lantern, the light of which emphasized the lines and crags of his face, his trimmed beard, and his grinning eyes. His tailored coat looked soft and rich, like velvet, and his breeches were leather. He might have seemed rich, but instead he seemed complicated, the richness of his clothes and the shining gold rings in his ears and chains on his neck contrasting with the worn leather of his gloves and boots. His thick, straight hair was tied in a tail with a red ribbon. He had a worn, well-used sword on a hanger at his belt—but the sword was missing the tip, the last six inches or so.

This was Edmund Blane.

You could lose a fencing bout before ever stepping onto the strip if you let your opponent intimidate you. If he had a reputation, and you let the reputation daunt you before the fight, you'd most likely lose. Fencing was as much a mind game as it was about physical skill.

She felt herself being daunted and tried to tell herself it was reputation, the stories she'd heard about him and fear left over from the battle at sea.

"Come along, then," he said in a soft, calm voice—a tone that surprised her, and made her even more wary. "We'll go where we can talk."

He turned and walked away, not waiting for her response, not caring if she had one. His men fell in around her, an obvious escort for a prisoner.

Well. This was what she'd wanted, wasn't it?

In silence, they continued. Blane and his crew didn't

seem to have the problem of not being able to walk in the straight line that Jill had struggled with. In moments, they left the forest and entered a rocky clearing.

Something crazy was going on, then. This was why no one could find them—unless Blane wanted to be found. Not that it made her feel any better.

In some ways, this seemed like a typical pirate camp, like the one that the *Diana*'s crew had made when they careened the ship on Jamaica. A pair of cook fires burned and formed the center of the camp; men were working repairing ropes, sails, tackle, any number of items; the smell of rum on the air was evident. But the atmosphere was subdued, taut. No one sang, no one laughed. They talked in low, anxious voices, and when Blane appeared they all fell silent and looked at him. Cooper's crew looked on her with respect when she passed by, maybe with fondness, maybe even some love, but always respect. Blane's crew turned wide and hungry eyes on him; they respected him and his power, but they obeyed him because they were afraid of him.

They were preparing weapons, sharpening blades on a whetstone, cleaning muskets and lining them up in a long, dark row.

Jill kept her back straight and reminded herself that she could use the sword she carried, that none of them had thought to take away from her. At least, she was pretty sure she could.

The clearing overlooked a cove, a sheltered inlet on the coast. The *Heart's Revenge* was anchored a little ways off, a fearsome ship lit by lanterns and flickering shadows, its masts naked and skeletal. Blane stopped at the edge of the camp, before the overhang dropped off, a steep slope to the narrow, sandy beach below, and looked out at his ship for a moment. Jill waited.

"Where is it?" Blane asked, still looking outward.

Jill swallowed; she hadn't had any water to drink in hours, and her throat was sticky. If she asked for a drink, they'd only give her something with rum in it. She wasn't going to drink any rum here.

"Where is what?" she said, knowing what he was asking about.

"The sword. You're here because you found the missing piece of my sword."

"How do you know that?"

"I made that sword. I know everything about it, and you're connected to it. Now, where's the shard?"

Even broken and useless, he still carried the sword because it was important. Because he needed it, and he needed it whole, because it had power. And if the broken piece of steel had brought her here, maybe the sword it had come from could send her home. Somehow.

Before she lost her nerve, she said quickly, "If you know everything, then you know how I got here, and you know I don't belong here. I need—I want to go back home. Can you help me? Can you send me back?"

"Perhaps. If you can tell me where the piece is."

It wasn't like he didn't already know so much, or that he could do anything differently if she told him. But saying where it was—telling him directly—would be betraying Captain Cooper. Jill couldn't do it.

"If you know everything about it, then you already know," she said, her voice shaking a little. She wasn't a very good liar. "Why ask me?"

He paced, hand hooked over the hilt of his sword, wry smile on his lips, polished boots crunching dirt underneath. "You could have lost it. You could have thrown it back into the sea. You could still have it. You could have given it to someone." He stopped and looked at her, eyebrows lifted. "Marjory Cooper?"

Jill didn't say anything.

"And she still has it? I'd have expected her to throw it back to the sea, as she did the last time. Can you tell me: Did she? Or did she keep it?"

He didn't know where it was. Otherwise, he wouldn't have fled the battle at sea last week. He'd have smashed the *Diana* to pieces, boarded her, and taken it. On some level, he must have been afraid of Cooper. Captain Cooper had stopped him last time by getting rid of the rapier shard. He was being careful because he didn't want her to do something like that again.

But he thought he could use Jill to get it.

"I don't know. Why would she tell me anything?" She tried to sound surly instead of scared.

"Because you're her protégé, I gather. Her apprentice. Why wouldn't she tell you?"

"I'm not anything to her," Jill said, and she wasn't entirely certain that was a lie.

"Oh, but you are, and you don't even know why, do you? She didn't tell you why you're so important, did she?" He laughed softly. "I know her. She's too soft. Her reputation says otherwise, but I know her."

Jill thought of Jenks and knew that Cooper wasn't soft. Blane didn't know her; he only thought he did. He was arrogant. "She hates you. She's looking for you."

"And you must not think much of her if you've come looking for me instead of keeping your lot in with her."

"I just want to go home," she said.

"My dear, what happened to you was a mistake and I'm sure I'm sorry for it. But I need that sword."

Maybe, she thought, Captain Cooper and the *Diana* hadn't been meant to fish her out of the ocean at all. Maybe, if Blane had been behind the bizarre time warp, he was supposed to find her first. Or if he hadn't caused it, he'd known that the shard had returned to his world. She'd emerged with it in that exact spot, where Blane had destroyed the *Newark*—had he been looking for her? Was she supposed to have been on the *Heart's Revenge* the whole time? As if there was a reason that all this was happening in the first place. She thought of what those first chaotic, confusing days had been like, and imagined herself among these men instead, without Abe's smile and Henry's joking. Blane's crew didn't seem to have any women among them at all.

She was glad that hadn't happened. She was glad the *Diana* had found her.

So what did she do now? She needed a moment to think.

"Why did you bring me here? Can you send me back or not?" she said. Tried to say with some authority, as if she could persuade him.

"I didn't bring you here," he said, amused. "I was simply looking for the piece of my sword."

But he couldn't have brought it back without someone hanging on to it—didn't he see that? It had been lying buried at the edge of the ocean for centuries without being washed back to him. He could have just brought it back—but someone had to carry it, and she was the one unlucky enough to pick it up. And now she was bound to it. She felt it like a touch in the back of her skull.

"I don't belong here," she said.

He looked at her askance, curious for the first time rather than just annoyed. "Just how far away did it land when Marjory threw it?"

"A long way away," Jill said quietly.

He wasn't going to help her. This had all been an accident, and she didn't have a part to play at all.

He studied his ship for another moment, then turned to her, donning a bright tone. Bright, but false. "Tell me— what is your name?"

"Jill," she said.

"Tell me, Jill—do you think Marjory will give me the piece in exchange for you? Would she do that to keep you safe?"

She didn't have to think about it. "No. I don't think she cares about me at all."

"Then I think we're done here," he said, and waved a gesture at her two guards.

They grabbed her arms and held tight. One of them held a rope he didn't have before, while the other wrenched her hands back. They bound her wrists behind her while she thrashed like a beached fish, uselessly.

They dragged her to the edge of the overlook, their intentions clear. With her hands free, able to reach out and brace herself or slow her fall, she might survive being thrown over the edge. Tied up, she'd tumble down until she broke.

She screamed, threw her weight back to try to anchor herself, but her two captors were stronger. Don't parry, she thought. Don't fall into a battle of strength—use your brain.

"Fight me!" she shouted, twisting to direct the words to Blane. "I challenge you to a duel! Fight me!"

Blane raised his hand, and the two men stopped their progress toward the edge. Jill slumped in their grasps and sighed. She'd bought herself a few more minutes, then. Maybe.

"You fight?" he said. "With a sword?"

"I'm not just wearing it for decoration," she said. "And I'm pretty good." That part was pure bluster.

But Blane took the bait, because he was arrogant. Jill read him right.

"Untie her."

One of the thugs drew a knife and sliced through the rope that bound her. She hissed when he nicked a piece of her skin; he didn't seem to notice.

They let her go. She backed away, trying to find a clear space, and drew her rapier. She spared a quick moment to wipe away blood from the heel of her left hand, where the knife had caught her.

Edmund Blane unfastened his belt, removing from his hip the broken sword that he wouldn't let out of his sight. Another of his men—they were all servants, interchangeable—was on hand to take the broken rapier and hand him another one. A whole, functional rapier with a worn grip and a sharp, gleaming blade. He held it up to his face, pointed outward, so he could gaze down the length of it, as if he didn't already know it was perfect. From the edge of her vision she watched the man who held the broken sword; he stood a little ways off but didn't leave the clearing, keeping the treasured rapier where Blane could see it.

The camp had fallen quiet. The men who had been working set aside their tools and gathered closer, to watch their captain fight the scrawny girl who'd appeared in their camp.

Jill was in something of a panic—she hadn't thought this through, she knew nothing about how Blane fought, it was dark, hard to see by wavering firelight, the ground was rocky, all of it about the worst conditions for a fight she could imagine. But at least she recognized that she was panicking. She might be able to at least stave it off before Blane ran her through—

No, he wasn't going to run her through; she wasn't going to let him. She breathed slowly, filling her lungs, set her body in a correct position, held her sword in a proper *en garde*. Habit and ritual steadied her. She shook out her legs, gave a little bounce to loosen her muscles, and looked toward Blane.

He watched her going through the motions, point of his rapier resting on the earth, opposite hand on his hip. His lips curled in a half smile.

She saluted him, bringing her sword straight up and flicking it away. He raised an eyebrow, and didn't salute her back.

For the first five heartbeats, neither of them moved. The tips of their rapiers barely crossed, which meant they were too far apart for either of them to make a real attack. This was just to size each other up. She made a beat—quickly tapping her blade against his. He didn't respond, merely letting his blade give to the pressure, then bringing it back on line. She tried again; this time, he disengaged, scooping his sword out of the way. She quickly responded by starting a parry—but he was only testing her, and he didn't take the opening. He didn't attack.

She couldn't believe how her heart was racing. She knew better than this; she didn't get nervous and sloppy before fights. He wasn't even doing anything to scare her—she was doing it all on her own. If she stayed scared, if she didn't do anything but stand here deciding what to do next, he'd pounce and she'd be dead.

Here and now, that wasn't just a figure of speech. The edge of his blade was sharp, and ended in a gleaming point.

He beat her blade, she beat back, and the fight was on. Attacking and counterattacking, he tested her. He was careful, calculating, his movements simple and precise. Textbook, which she wasn't sure she'd expected from someone who by all accounts was a hardened villain. Maybe she'd expected the sweeping, flailing attacks of a movie swashbuckler. But Edmund Blane had had training, and he practiced. He drew her responses, and she fell into the expected pattern, as if they were drilling. She was dancing to the tune he played.

She stumbled back, out of his reach, to break out of the pattern and reassess. She circled, aware of Blane's followers around the torch-lit clearing where they fought. They could strike at any moment as well.

So she brought the fight to him, lunging in a feint, countering the parry she expected. He matched her, with a bare smile and a gleam in his eyes. Good fencing wasn't just hitting; it was a conversation, move and countermove, anticipating three or more movements along until each exchange was comprised of a dozen moves or more, steel on steel ringing out. The familiar fire lit in her veins, flowed through her limbs, and her muscles found their rhythm.

This was a good fight. She just wished the swords weren't real. Her mind felt electric, otherworldly—she'd rather be watching this from the outside.

After two or three complex exchanges, she decided she could hold her own against him—for a time. If she played a purely defensive game, concentrated on blocking, didn't take risks. But if she did that, she'd never stop him. He'd wear her out, eventually she would make a mistake, and he would finish her.

She had to get out of this. So she turned and ran.

No one ran after her, probably because they were shocked. Even Blane stood and stared. Jill planned—however much she planned any of this—to just keep running, to plunge into the forest and escape. But the man charged with holding Blane's broken rapier stood in her path. If she stopped, if she lost her momentum, Blane would have her thrown over the cliff—nothing would change. This wasn't a feint; she was committed. She kept going, arms bent, still holding her rapier, charging forward.

The man in front of her flinched. And maybe that brief show of fear inspired Jill. She felt a surge, the flicker of a smile on her lips—she recognized the feeling, that moment when she saw an opening, recognizing an opponent's weakness. The broken sword was Edmund Blane's weakness.

She ran into the pirate, shouldering him out of the way,

and grabbed the sword out of his hands. The sword caught; she felt it drag through flesh. The man screamed as a wound opened on his hand where the blade cut, and he stumbled away from her. She kept running, never slowing, keeping her eyes where she wanted to go—the shadows in the forest beyond.

Other pirates were running now, moving to intercept her and capture her. Blane might even have been yelling. Jill had her task and didn't waver; all she had to do was run. So she did, a sword in each hand, and let the shadows of the forest devour her.

The noise she made—the breaking of branches, the crashing of foliage—sounded immense to her ears. She'd never be able to hide or escape, because the whole forest knew she was here. She only had one chance at this. The voices shouting after her seemed close, echoing all around her—surely surrounding her. But the pirates didn't catch her.

When she traveled this path previously, she felt she'd been walking in circles. Now the way seemed clear. It was as if she'd walked in a fog before, but now the fog had lifted. Whatever Blane had done to keep wanderers from finding his camp was gone. Or maybe—she was the one who held his sword now. Maybe it was the sword.

And now it was Jill's, and maybe it really could help her get home.

Whatever had happened to the metaphysical fog that made her lose her way when she passed through here last time, she still had to contend with the forest itself, its tangle of vegetation, crawling vines, and jutting branches. She couldn't pick her way and choose her path; she just ran and shoved her way past obstacles, letting them claw and scratch at her. The wounds stung, a sheen of sweat covered her, and her whole body felt sticky. It was too hot to breathe. She expected that at any moment she'd hear a musket fire, and that Blane would be standing behind her, shooting her dead. She ran as if she could outrun the sound of gunfire.

"Hey! Oy there!" The shout came from off to her left; the speaker was hidden in shadow and foliage. Jill automatically veered away.

"Get her! She's here!" another voice said, this one right in front of her, and she realized too late that she'd fallen for a trick, and the voices meant to steer her where they could best capture her. It probably didn't matter where she ran now.

She kept on, shoving her way past shrubs and branches that seemed intent on catching her and holding her.

Suddenly, so quickly she stumbled at the freedom of it, she left the forest and entered open country near the edge of Nassau. And standing before her were Henry, Abe, and Captain Cooper. Jill stared, gasping for breath, disbelieving. Behind her, two more of the crew tore out of the trees. They looked hot and sweaty and were brushing dirt and debris off themselves. Jill, holding back a sob of relief, wondered how long they'd been chasing after her.

Henry looked like he'd been running, trying to catch his breath. He had his sword drawn and grasped it like he was anxious for a fight.

"God, Jill!" he said. "You're all right! You an't hurt!"

She wasn't sure that was entirely true, but she was here and alive. She nodded, sheepish at the panic. He went on, still desperate. "When I'd heard you were after Blane, I thought—you were gone, we'd find you hacked to pieces and that would be the end of it. Are you barmy, are you trying to get yourself killed?"

He was truly worried about her. All his joking had disappeared, and if he really had found her dead, he would have gone after Blane himself, and Blane would have thrown him over the cliff, too.

Jill stared at him. If they'd been alone, if they hadn't both been holding swords, she would have flung herself at him and kissed him.

Instead, before Jill could do anything, Captain Cooper smiled and let out a sigh. She said, "Bloody hell, you've got his sword."

13

PASSÉ

They moved quickly from the woods back to Nassau and to the wharf. Arranged like a military squadron, Cooper and Abe in the lead; Tennant and Matthews behind, pistols drawn, keeping watch; Henry stayed at Jill's elbow, gazing outward like he expected demons to attack them. And maybe Blane really could send demons after them.

Cooper let her keep the broken sword. Jill slung her own, whole rapier back in its hanger on her belt, and held the broken one in sweaty hands.

"What happened back there?" Henry asked. "What the blazes were you *doing*?"

"I thought maybe Blane would know how to get me home," she said, weakly, sad now that the thought had ever occurred to her.

"So what happened? Did you find him? Obviously you found him, or at least his sword. Did you talk to him? What did he—"

"I challenged him to a duel," Jill said, wincing.

"Bloody hell, you did not," Henry said. His lip curved, a hint of his usual smile. "Please tell me you killed him dead."

"No. I ran. I guess that makes me a coward."

"Never!" Henry said, laughing. "Real pirates always run from fights, and I knew you were a real pirate the moment we fished you out of the drink."

"Captain, look ahead there," Abe said, holding out an arm to stop the company. He nodded ahead but didn't point. Jill saw a small group of men, four or five of them, pistols drawn, emerge from an alley ahead, looking back and forth, searching.

"Right, this way," Cooper said, turning to cut through the yard of a squat clapboard building, a maze of rotten coils of rope and broken timbers. The way was dark; Jill couldn't see the ground more than a few feet before her, and every step was treacherous. Single file, the group picked a path through the debris, past the building, and out of view of their pursuers.

They made their way to a rocky shore.

"They'll be watching the pier," Cooper said. "Abe and Tennant, bring us a rowboat and we'll try to sneak out from under them. Matthews, go through the town, get everyone back on the ship. We've got to fly and we only have a little time before the tide turns against us. Anyone who's left is left. Go!" The men ran.

The remaining three of them waited, backs together, looking out in all directions. Henry and Cooper had pistols drawn, and Jill suddenly felt defenseless with only two swords. A sword and a half, really.

Captain Cooper took the opportunity to berate her. "What did you think you were doing then, running off on me like that? Going to sell me out to my enemy then? Deserting the ship and going turncoat?"

"I don't know what I was doing," Jill said, sullen. "You didn't seem to care all that much about what happened to me, so I had to take care of myself."

"By running to Blane?" she said, scowling.

"If he brought me here, even by mistake, he ought to know how to send me home, right?"

"And what did the man do, then? Apologize and offer to send you home straight away?" Cooper said.

"No. He was going to throw me off a cliff."

"There, you see?"

"But I got his sword," Jill said.

They were glaring at each other, with Henry to the side, looking back and forth between them. Cooper grumbled at him. "What are you staring at, whelp?"

"Um . . ." Henry's eyes went wide and he pointed his pistol past Cooper's shoulder. "Look there!"

Henry fired; Jill and Cooper dropped to the ground. The shot sounded like a miniature cannon, an echoing pop. The smell of burned gunpowder was the same.

There were two of the enemies hiding behind a tower of barrels at the end of the block. Jill was pretty sure Henry had missed, because they leaned out, stealing looks, waving their own pistols—and firing. Puffs of white smoke rose up. Jill covered her head, but they missed as well. The three of them took shelter behind their own pile of crates and debris.

Cooper fired next while Henry reloaded, which required ramming powder and ammunition down the barrel of the weapon. Her targets ducked back without being hit. Blane's men fired a second time and missed again.

This could go on all night.

"Here, girl. Keep them distracted." Cooper put the pistol in her hand and ran, disappearing around the street corner.

"I don't know what to do with this," she hissed at Henry.

"Here. You fire, I'll reload." He handed her his own pistol and took Cooper's empty one from her.

How hard could it be? Especially since the pistols didn't seem able to hit anything. She sighted down the barrel and waited for one of the targets to appear.

Half a face emerged and a pistol fired toward her. Jill pulled the trigger—the brass mechanism on top of the pistol snapped forward and the weapon fired, jumping in her hand. A cloud of white smoke expanded and partially blinded her. She coughed and waved it out of her face.

The two men were still there, still firing. Her shot probably flew out over the harbor. She huffed in frustration. She hated missing.

"Next shot," Henry said, handing her Cooper's newly loaded pistol and taking the empty from her.

She repeated her fencing mantra. Stay calm, keep breathing, don't panic. She just had to be careful and take her time.

From around the stack of barrels, a pistol appeared again, its owner leaning out to take aim. Jill exhaled and squeezed her finger. The pistol jumped, burned with fire, and the cloud of smoke burst into her face.

And at the other end of the block, a man screamed.

"Oh, good work, Jill!" Henry said, laughing.

She couldn't believe it, but when the smoke cleared, one

of Blane's men had fallen, gripping his arm and cursing. His companion started to drag him back to cover, when he twitched back—and Captain Cooper was there, slicing a dagger across his throat. Blood poured, and he fell, hands on his neck, hopelessly trying to stop the flow. Then he lay still.

Cooper put her boot on the chest of the man Jill had shot and leaned over to cut his throat as well. The two had been so distracted by Jill and Henry firing at them, they hadn't noticed their killer sneaking up behind.

The two bodies lay there, blood dripping from them and soaking into the ground. Jill could almost smell it, sharp and bitter against the dank sea air. Her stomach clenched, and she pressed her hand over her mouth and turned away. After a moment of shallow breathing her stomach settled and her racing heart calmed. The battle was one thing; the blood spilled then had happened too quickly to really process. This was different. She could see their eyes, open and staring at nothing. This looked like murder—even if the men had been trying to kill them. Cooper had slit their throats, and that wasn't self-defense, was it? What, then, was the difference between a duel and murder?

Her heart racing, Jill wasn't sure how she felt about this battle in miniature. It didn't seem right, none of it. Even if they'd had every intention of killing her and her friends. But she'd never seen anyone die before.

She preferred baited blades and no blood.

"You all right, then?" Henry asked. Jill just shook her head.

Cooper returned to them, wiping off her dagger with a handkerchief.

"Here comes Abe with the rowboat," the captain said.

Abe and Tennant ran the boat ashore, and the others climbed in, splashing in the waves and pushing off. Henry and Abe took the oars, and in moments they were slipping across the harbor. Skillfully, the two cut the water without a splash, with barely a ripple. Cooper stood at the prow of the boat, scanning forward. The harbor was quiet.

"I wish I knew where Blane's bloody ship was. I fear he's circling just outside the harbor, waiting for us to sail out so he can pounce on us," Cooper said. "We'll get to the *Diana* and make our escape for nothing."

"He's anchored in a cove to the east," Jill said. "He's got a camp there. I don't think he can get here to catch us in time."

"I don't know, lass. Blane's got tricky ways about him, and he'll want that sword back." Now she grinned. "That must have been quite a sight, you taking it from him."

"Honestly, it was kind of a blur," Jill said.

"Probably for the best. Where's my crew? Who's on watch?" Cooper whistled, and a figure appeared at the gunwales. A moment later a line came over the side, and the boat was secured to the *Diana*.

They waited for the rest of the crew to return, another long, dragging hour. Jill understood the captain's worry. Logically, Blane was on the other side of the island and couldn't reach them. Nonetheless, Jill expected to see the *Heart's Revenge* blazing into the harbor at any moment, all its cannons firing.

It didn't happen.

Back on board, Jill followed Captain Cooper and Abe to her cabin, where the two of them started pulling charts from a drawer. The group of them gathered over the table, a conspiracy bent under the light of a single lantern: Captain Cooper and Abe, looking grim and serious; Jill and Henry, who hadn't left Jill's side since they found her running through the forest away from Blane.

"We make for the Turks and Caicos, then on to the Lesser Antilles," Marjory said, pointing, before Jill had even oriented herself. The maps were rough, the lines jagged, the labels scrawled in indecipherable handwriting. The paper itself was stained and wrinkled; these maps had seen better days. "We lose ourselves. Stay far away from where Blane expects to find us. We've got to keep this away from him.

Let's see it, then." Cooper gestured at the broken sword Jill still held close.

The captain could have overpowered Jill, simply taken it, and left her behind to whatever fate. But she didn't. Jill had kept the sword tucked away and safe during the escape from Nassau. Now she brought it into the faint, flickering light.

The swept hilt was simple and elegant, smooth steel bars looping to form a cage around the hand that gripped it. Quillons stuck out, perpendicular to the wire-wrapped grip. The blade was broad and strong, sharpened until light seemed to spark off the edge. It was fierce and perfect, until the end, which was a jagged, toothy stump.

Cooper reached into a pouch at her belt and drew out the six-inch scrap of rapier Jill had found on that long-ago beach, roughly cleaned, the edges dull. The length of steel trembled, pulling against her fingers, drawn toward the sword as it had been all along. The captain kept a firm hold on it as she brought it to the sword and lined them together.

The ragged edges matched. Cooper fit them together, and not a sliver of steel was missing between them. The scrollwork design that the rusted piece hinted at continued, shining, on the main blade. The sword, though, remained broken. The pieces matched, but didn't fuse. The magic didn't go that far.

The captain looked at Jill. "Many years ago, Edmund

Blane betrayed me. We fought. I broke his sword and threw the piece overboard. I thought it was lost forever. Then you came along. Now I know that wasn't the end of it and my job isn't done yet."

"How did he betray you?" Jill asked.

"He told me he loved me." Captain Cooper ducked her gaze for a moment, and a wry smile played on her lips. "Ah, but that was just the start of it. It's a very dark story, against all nature and reason. A difficult story to tell."

The room was silent; even the groaning of lines and the wooden hull seemed muted. The others listened—maybe they'd never heard the story, either.

Marjory Cooper gathered herself to tell it. "There are places in these islands where folk practice dark magic— black magic and blood sacrifice. Blane twisted that magic. He told me he loved me, see, and we had a child together. A little girl. Wee Jenny."

Jill's breath caught. Abe sighed. "Captain, he—"

"Oh yes, Abe, he did," Cooper said. "He made himself a sword and quenched it in her blood. All for the power it brought him, no matter how dark." Her voice had turned soft, and her look numb. No feeling entered her telling of the tale. And how could it? How could she let herself feel it without going mad?

Then she straightened, smiled sadly, and was human for

a moment. She nodded at Jill. "She'd be just about your age now, if she had lived. However you found it I think that shard of rapier called to you. Somehow, the blood on it called to you, and called to Blane. Somehow, because of who you are—who you might have been, who my little girl might have been—you're bound to that sword."

Jill looked at everything that had happened these past weeks through new eyes, which stung with the tragedy of it. Cooper had become a different person. She studied the sword in her hand, and now saw all that it symbolized. A whole history of betrayal. It was more than cursed. Turning it in the light, Jill could almost see a sheen of red on the blade, tinting the steel. How had she ever thought this sword could help her? How could any of it be possible?

Her voice cracking, Jill said, "I'm not your daughter, Captain."

"I know, love. But I can dream that she'd have been like you, can't I?"

Abe took up the story: "Blane is building a fleet—he would have every pirate captain under his sway. He would have them all swear allegiance to him by this cursed sword, and then they would be bound to him, and he would be a pirate emperor. The captain broke the sword rather than let that happen."

"He speaks of a pirate alliance—but wants a pirate

empire, and he'll cut down all who oppose him," Cooper said.

"And what will you do with the sword?" Jill asked.

"Part of me thinks I could use it to build a fleet to oppose Blane. But I could never use this power, knowing where it came from. How Blane does it—" She ended, shaking her head.

"But pirates aren't meant to sail in fleets, are they?" Jill asked.

"Some of them have, like Captains Avery and Morgan," Abe said. "But such alliances never last long. They're alliances, not armies. A pirate ought only be bound by the articles he signs and the vote of the ship."

"Except for Blane, who hasn't any honor at all," Cooper said.

"Blane thinks he can bind pirate honor up in an object, in a thing, like that sword," Abe said.

"We should get rid of the damned thing," Henry said. "Throw it into the sea, if it would really give him that power."

Jill resisted an urge to pull the sword away from them. "What about me? What if it could send me home?"

After a long, silent moment, Cooper met Jill's gaze, as intent as Jill had ever seen her. "If it can be done, we will learn how and do it. And if it can't—you'll have a place among us here until the end of all our days."

"Pirates don't tend to live all that long, do they?" Jill said. Cooper turned away.

Tennant leaned in through the doorway. "Boat ahoy, sir."

"There it is, then. When everyone's on board, we run. And keep it quiet." Cooper looked at her. "Jill, lass, will you let me lock the sword up? Blane can't ever find it. If he got hold of it and the shard together, he'd have all the power he wants."

"You won't get rid of it without telling me?" Jill said.

"You have my word."

Pirate honor. Jill believed her, and set the rapier in the trunk. The captain locked it and gave Jill the key. "Blane will never have this, will he?"

"No, sir," Jill said. Cooper returned the broken tip to her belt pouch. "Not like I need it to find Blane now, when he'll come find us."

The flight began.

As soon as the other rowboat appeared, the crew on board the schooner began setting sails. Jill climbed into the rigging with them to unfurl sails and secure lines, while others began raising anchor. By the time the last rowboat was secured, the ship was underway.

Jill wouldn't have guessed it was possible, but the *Diana* sailed away from Nassau unnoticed, with all her crew aboard. Abe hissed his commands, the crew scrambled to their positions, and sails unfolded like petals on a flower at dawn. Water splashed, wood creaked, lines and canvas snapped, but all the ships at anchor shifted, creaked, and moaned, restless murmurs on an ever-moving sea. The tide and a cool night breeze were with them. The current flowed out to sea, tugging the schooner with it, and the wind pushed them along. By lantern light and hushed voices, they left the town with its boisterous parties and blazing taverns—and Edmund Blane's plots—behind.

The wind was with them, and the seas were calm. They couldn't have asked for a better escape. It seemed a good omen. Jill imagined Blane still onshore, his men hunting through the forest for her; or maybe he stood on the shore at Nassau, watching his rapier and his enemies sailing away.

Or maybe, and this was probably most likely, he was hoisting sails on his own ship to give chase.

14

STOP THRUST

It must have been close to midnight; the moon was sinking toward the west, and Jill was too nervous to sleep. Her eyes ached with exhaustion, but when she lay down in a hammock belowdecks, her head rang with imagined noises—the flick of steel against steel, distant cannon fire. If she slept, Blane would slit her throat. If he was going to kill her, she would be on her feet, giving him a run for his money when he did.

Maybe she was getting used to being a pirate after all.

She went up on deck to watch the waves, hoping the view would help her relax and make her headache go away. At the prow, she felt the full breeze of their passage, away from the shelter of the sails. Leaning on the edge, she felt like she was flying. It was almost a perfect moment, sitting near the bowsprit of a schooner under full sail, plowing through the waves of an open sea. She licked her lips to taste the salt spray and tipped her head back to let the wind tangle her hair. Above, sails framed a diamond-studded sky. She could forget why she was here, and that she didn't belong. She'd forget it all for the moment.

Henry cleared his throat, startling her. The noise was a warning, to let her know that he approached, inching along the gunwales, asking by gesture—slouched shoulders and a sheepish expression—if he could join her. She didn't say anything, trying not to let on that he'd surprised her, and her muscles had tensed back to fighting readiness. He settled himself near her, close enough to reach out to her, but far enough to let her scramble out of the way if he tried. She'd never seen him so skittish.

"Hi," she said to break the tension. His anxiety was making her more nervous.

"Hullo," he said. A few more moments passed; Jill listened to the waves slapping against the hull and felt the familiar rolling of the ship.

"You all right, then?" Henry said.

"Did you know?" she asked. "About Captain Cooper, and

what Blane did to her." And their child, their little girl . . . That sword was haunted, Jill knew now.

Henry shook his head. "No, none of us knew, not even Abe, and they've been sailing together forever. We didn't know why she hated Blane, only that she did."

"It's awful," she said. The words seemed so inadequate.

"Aye," he said. "It's an awful thing."

"If I'd known before, when I challenged him—I'd have been too scared."

"And if you face him again?"

She sighed. "I don't know."

"How are you, then?"

She pursed her lips, trying to figure out how to answer. For the moment, she was fine. But she didn't know what she was going to do when the sun rose. She could only shake her head.

"Is it really so bad here?" Henry said, sounding pained. "Do you really want so much to leave?"

"It isn't that, it's just—" She almost reached out to him. Almost took his arms and held him—and she almost didn't want to go. "I'm not supposed to be here. I've got to get back home."

He said, "If I don't understand, it's because, you see—I'm sure you've seen—that most of us don't have anything to go back for. This is all the family we have, and all the world we need. Heaven and hell together." He gazed up and around, taking in masts and sails, starry sky, sea and horizon all.

She kissed him. Leaned forward, almost without looking, dug her fingers into his shoulders and put her lips on his. She took him by surprise, completely. The first moment, she pressed against him while he held himself rigid. But then he melted, his arms closing around her, his face leaning in, his lips moving against hers in a warm, salt-tasting kiss.

After a moment, he pulled away. They studied each other, eyes only inches apart, so it wasn't as if they could really see each other. For her part, Jill saw enough.

"I'm glad I met you, Henry," she said.

"I—" Then he ducked his gaze and smiled. "You're a rare one, and for all the pain it's caused you, I'm glad we met as well."

"I just wish I knew what was going to happen."

"You still don't understand, do you? It's not about what happens. We all may be dead next week, eh? It's about what you've got now. The wind and the sea. A bottle of rum and a ship of your own. Don't think about what happens next."

"Is that really a good way to live?"

He looked out at the water and avoided her searching gaze. His smile was gone now, and she was sorry she'd said anything to make it disappear. "No, it an't a good way to live. It's a good way to die, in fact. I suppose you'd have me go ashore and live an honest working life."

She tried to imagine Henry as a workman onshore, one of the laborers in the harbor, loading and unloading other people's cargo all day. She couldn't.

"It's not my place to tell you to do anything," she said.

He touched her cheek and kissed her forehead. "Right now, we'll sit and watch the waves. Then we'll see what happens tomorrow. Eh?"

She could argue 'til morning, and he'd still be right.

Dawn broke with gray and pink streaking the sky, and the sight of a three-masted ship on the horizon, matching them for direction and speed.

"It's him. The *Heart's Revenge*," Captain Cooper said, lowering the spyglass from her eye. "I don't know how, we had a full night's lead and were racing."

"We still have a lead on 'em," Abe said. "We'll lose the bugger."

"Aye, we will. Make sail!"

So the race commenced.

Jill would have thought hiding would be easy on a vast, huge ocean. A person swimming, tiny and lost among the waves, certainly would vanish. A ship could sail for weeks on the open ocean and never see another, never see land. Yet a pirate ship could always find prey on common shipping lanes; piracy thrived in the Caribbean because the sea was crowded with islands rich with trade. The ocean could be deceptively crowded. And they couldn't escape Blane's ship.

A chase by large sailing ship wasn't just a matter of setting sails and hoping. This wasn't like the steady cruising of previous days. Cooper kept close watch on Blane's ship, trying to guess his strategy, to judge how his ship was handling and how he was riding the wind. The crew attended to the *Diana*, making constant adjustments based on changes in the wind, trimming sails and tightening lines to best take advantage of their only source of power. They knew what they were doing and were good at their job; the *Diana* traveled lightly over the waves. Silver-skinned dolphins played in their wake, leaping and diving, mindless of the drama taking place between the two ships.

On watch, Jill spent part of the day on the rigging of the mainmast, waiting to take in the line to trim one of the sails. Around noon the ship changed direction and began tacking, a complicated operation that changed which side of the ship took the brunt of the wind. Booms swung across the deck, triangular sails flapped uselessly for a moment, and Abe shouted orders. In seconds, the sails grew taut again and the ship jumped forward, heeling over, then leaning into her new course. Manning the sails was difficult, precarious work, but there was satisfaction in being part of a crew, of helping to control the ship to ride the winds.

The course change confused Blane, and they lost sight of him for part of the day; the *Heart's Revenge* didn't tack as sharply and neatly as the *Diana* did, and he had to loop around. Captain Cooper didn't pause to appreciate the small victory, but ordered them to maintain full sails and racing speed, still bound for the chain of islands east of the Bahamas.

Before dusk fell, the lookout cried out and pointed—there it was, that ship bobbing into view on the far horizon, white sails gleaming, catching the last rays of sun that cut across the ocean.

"Bloody hell, how's he doing it?" Abe said.

Cooper watched him through the spyglass a moment before turning to him. "Have we got anything else we can put up?"

"Every inch of canvas we have is already set, Captain," he answered. "Even if we had more we can't go any faster without breaking to pieces."

"Damn. Well then, looks like we may have a fight on our hands after all."

The crew who weren't on the rigging, manning the sails, or helping with the ship, spent the time cleaning and loading muskets, pistols, and making the cannons ready. No longer sure they could outrun Blane, they prepared for battle. Jill cleaned and sharpened her borrowed rapier, which seemed dull and useless.

None of them slept that night. Around what must have been midnight, Jill found Captain Cooper still at the helm, still watching behind them. Blane's ship, lit by lanterns, was visible as a faint glow, like a star come to rest on the waves.

"What are we going to do when he catches up with us?" Jill asked. She'd moved quietly, didn't announce herself, but Cooper didn't seem startled when she spoke.

"We'll make our stand, I suppose," Cooper said, a little too fatalistically, a little too willing to give in to the inevitable.

"We can't win against him," Jill said. "How many cannons does he have? A dozen?"

"Twenty," Cooper said, and Jill imagined her counting each one on their last encounter, and knowing exactly what that many cannons on a ship that size could do if it cornered a schooner like the *Diana*. "But we have speed. We can keep ahead of him, just watch."

"But we'll have to stop eventually, and he'll find us."

"Here now, who's been at sea half her life and knows far more about it than you, you wee tadpole?"

It sounded like bluster. Cooper could be standing with a sword at her throat and she'd never admit she was beaten. Blane's ship was bigger, better armed, with more crew. All the *Diana* had was speed, and if that didn't work—

Well, no. They had something else that Blane didn't—both pieces of the cursed sword. And Cooper had *her*, her and the sword together, which Blane had never had.

She almost hated to bring it up. "You said you'd thought about using Blane's sword."

Cooper huffed and shook her head. "It's cursed. Haunted. I can't even tell you all that sword's about."

"What would happen if we fixed it? Put the two pieces back together."

"That's what Blane wants. No, we can't do it." Cooper bowed her head so her thick hair fell over her shoulders. Hiding some expression. When she looked up again, her expression was cold. "If we repair the sword and Blane gets ahold of it again, we're done for. I'll not have that. I ought to bury both pieces on different islands and watch him scramble."

Jill took a breath. "If I have that sword, I think I can beat him."

The words shocked her—she was sure she hadn't meant to say that. Then she thought, maybe that was it. Maybe fighting Blane—and winning, beating him with his own power—would send her home. It made sense: The only thing that would defeat Edmund Blane was Edmund Blane's own power, his own curse, confronting him with the blood he'd spilled. She remembered the feeling of the sword in her hand, the sensation of leather and wood against her palm, and she knew it had power. Her hands itched to hold the sword, whole and ready for fighting, again. Even if it was haunted.

Rather than refusing and cursing at her, Cooper considered. Jill couldn't guess what the captain was thinking when she looked at her with that narrowed gaze.

"You faced Blane, didn't you? You fought him?"

"Yes, sir," Jill said.

"You aren't lying about it."

"No, sir."

"And you held your own against him?"

"I didn't beat him, but I didn't lose, either."

"And what makes you think you can beat him now?" she demanded.

"It's the sword. Not by myself, but with that sword." She had to try. . . .

Then Cooper shook her head. "It sounds all high and mighty, but we can't risk getting close enough to Blane to see if you're right. Now get up on the mainmast and take the next watch."

Jill almost argued. She had stood up to Blane, however briefly; standing up to Captain Cooper ought to be easier. She was planted on the deck, her jaw stiff with the arguments she wanted to make—if the sword had power, couldn't they use it, too? They glared at each other, neither of them flinching, Cooper daring her to make a challenge and Jill almost doing it. But unlike facing Blane back on the island, she didn't have anywhere to run to on the ship.

Jill marched to the mainmast, where she swung into the rigging and pulled herself to the lookout perch, working out her frustration through her muscles.

Looking out over the ocean, a tiny sphere of lantern light reflected on distant water. The *Heart's Revenge*, still trailing them.

At some point near dawn, Jill stumbled down off the mainmast, clinging to ropes while half asleep and nearly missing a couple of her grips. She was too tired and angry to be frightened by her near misses. She made it belowdecks and into a hammock and must have slept for an hour or so. Noises above deck and sunlight coming in through the hatch awakened her.

Startled, she swung out of the hammock, half falling, and looked for a sword or pistol, sure that the battle had started. But no, there hadn't been any cannon fire. No one shouted in a panic. The deck above echoed with the sound of something being hauled across it, and of Captain Cooper calling out orders.

Jill climbed up on deck and blinked in the sunlight.

In a clear space in the middle of the deck, a large crate had been set, and cannonballs stacked in the crate. Nearby, members of the crew were breaking up other crates, building a pile of splintered wood.

"What's going on?" Jill said. Of all the strangeness she'd seen and learned since arriving on the *Diana*, this made the least sense.

Abe, who had been walking along the deck, smiled at her. "We're going to build a fire without burning down the ship. What do you think?"

Jill shook her head. "Why?"

"You'll see. You'll like it."

She could only stare, baffled.

Then Captain Cooper joined them. "Tadpole, you'll need to get Blane's sword from the chest. We're going to see about mending it."

15

FORTE

The crew had a former blacksmith among them—
Tennant, it turned out. But before they could mend
the sword, they had to see about building a makeshift forge
on the deck of the *Diana*—without damaging the ship. They
didn't dare put into land on one of the scattered islands.
Blane would reach them before they'd even brought the
equipment to shore. They had to keep moving.

They managed to build a forge using the stove from
the galley and cannonballs to protect the deck. Tennant lit
the fire and put crew to work keeping it stoked.

Hands trembling, Jill fetched the sword from the captain's

strongbox. As the weapon came into the light, the steel seemed to gleam more brightly, light singing off the edge. She ran a finger along the flat of the blade, then along the curve of the hilt. Trying to feel any power coming off it, listening for some message. It may have been her imagination that the metal had a reddish tinge. She couldn't help but think of the story behind the sword, and she almost dropped it back into the trunk. Maybe Cooper was right, and they should just get rid of it.

But what if it really was the key?

On deck, Captain Cooper met her near the forge, now blazing with heat, and produced the broken tip of the blade.

"I'm still not sure this is the right thing to do," Cooper said.

Jill glanced at the sword and her heart ached. This was all she could think of. The alternative was running away, farther and farther from where she belonged with every mile.

"I'm not sure, either," she admitted. "But we have to try."

"Aye," the captain said. Then her lips turned in the smile she donned before battle. "We'll finish the ruddy bastard off once and for all. What say you, ready to give Blane's sword back to him point first?"

The crew cheered. Jill raised the broken sword and shouted with them.

They gave the two pieces to Tennant, who seemed daunted, his lips pursed and grim. The gunnery mate used a tong to set the lengths of steel into the stove, then stripped off his shirt and tied it around his waist.

A barrel of water waited nearby, secured to the mast to keep it steady, in case a fire broke out.

Meanwhile, the rest of the crew worked to keep the ship away from Blane and the *Heart's Revenge* for as long as it took to repair the sword.

Captain Cooper steered them into a network of islands, part of some ancient mountain range where only the peaks emerged from the water. Navigating around the verdant, jutting islands and reefs slowed their progress, but Blane would have a harder time following them. So Cooper hoped, and for a time the *Heart's Revenge* fell behind. They hid behind islands, then changed their course, hoping to be well ahead by the time Blane realized he was going the wrong way.

"He'll loop around the whole mess, I'll wager, catch us as we come out of this," Abe said, his hands tight on the wheel at the helm, watching the path carefully. Several of the crew kept watch, shouting out directions and noting obstacles, reefs and sandbars.

"Perhaps. But to do that he's got to guess where we'll come out," Cooper said.

Jill wondered if Blane could sense his sword. He wouldn't

have to guess, he'd just know where it was and feel it traveling toward him.

Over a dinner of boiled stew and hard bread, sitting near the bowsprit, Jill told Henry her fears.

After considering a moment, Henry said, "If such a thing were possible, Blane could do it."

"Then it doesn't matter what we do. He'll always find us, and he'll overpower us no matter what."

"You told the captain you could beat him using that sword," he said.

"But I don't know if I can," she admitted. Saying it aloud seemed to make her losing the fight more likely, and she suddenly lost her appetite.

"Then it was a trick," he said after a moment. "You just want the sword because you think it'll get you out of here, and it isn't about Blane at all."

"No, that's not true." At least, she didn't think it was true. She couldn't look at him.

"Look, if you don't think you can beat him, you shouldn't fight him," Henry said.

"You'd have to be brilliant to beat him," she said, thinking back to the one fight, trying to pick apart his style. He'd been toying with her. It wasn't enough for her to have a strong defense. She had to be able to counterattack. "He's fast and smart—I tried to attack, but he always seemed to know exactly what I was doing, where I was going to put my sword, even before I knew, like he could read my mind. Henry, he's really good."

"I know I wouldn't want to fight him. I couldn't beat him. He's never lost a duel."

Jill had been in tournaments with fencers whose reputations preceded them, where the whispers passed through locker rooms and along team benches. *She's never been beaten, she's never lost a bout.* And if you listened to those rumors you'd already lost. This was the same, Jill thought.

As much as this was about skill and talent, this was a mind game.

The crew kept to the edges of the ship, against the sides, away from the heat and noise in the center of the deck. Tennant was still working, hammering at the sword, steel on steel. The noise of it rattled above the snapping of sails and splash of waves.

The ship rounded a spit of island as the sun set, turning the ocean a molten pewter color. Tennant still hammered at the sword, and Jill wished this didn't have to take so long. It wasn't just a matter of gluing one piece of steel to another—the tip would only break off again the first time she hit anything. Tennant had to reforge the blade. Get the steel hot enough that it became malleable, so that the two pieces could be hammered together, merged, making the molecular structure of the metal continuous. When he was finished, if he knew what he was doing, the break wouldn't simply be mended—it would vanish, as if it had never been, and the blade would be as strong as ever.

Then she could fight with it.

Jill had been trying to sleep on deck—no one was lingering belowdecks, except the surgeon, who was still locked in his closet. No one was sleeping much, either. People kept looking over the water for the *Heart's Revenge*. When the night turned still, with only the waves and sails as background noise, Jill needed a moment to notice, for the clanging of hammer on steel to fade from her ears. Tennant had finished.

She clambered to her feet and raced to the central deck. Tennant was holding the sword tip-down in the barrel of water. The fire in the forge was flickering out.

"It's done?" she asked.

He glanced at her. Even in the cool breeze, his whole body was slick with sweat, his tan skin shining with it, his trousers soaked through. The scarf tied around his head, meant to keep sweat out of his eyes, was itself dripping. His shoulders dropped, weary, and his smile was weak. But he smiled.

"Not quite yet, lass. The blade needs an edge."

Jill sighed. Behind them, the shadow of an island loomed, painted charcoal under the light of the stars and moon. The *Heart's Revenge* was on the other side, presumably coming around to chase them down.

"There isn't time," she said.

"The Captain'll keep us ahead of the dog, just you see." Tennant left the sword cooling in the barrel, then went to sit down and take a long drink from a mug.

At dawn, she climbed the mainmast to keep the next watch. The island they'd passed in the night was a haze on the horizon; the next was approaching to starboard, and Cooper was plotting a course that would take them around the windward side of it.

Jill called down when the *Heart's Revenge* came into view. All its sails were hoisted, a vast field of white gleaming in the rising sun.

"How's it coming, Tennant?" the captain called. The smith was on deck, working to sharpen the blade, polishing the edge with a stone.

"Need more time, sir!" he called back. Their voices were distant, echoing. Jill felt removed from it all, drifting above the ships and the action. Now if she could just float away. . . .

"Right, let's keep the bastard running!"

The ship tipped until Jill was hanging over the water, and

she tightened her grip on the rope. If she fell, she'd hit the waves instead of the *Diana*'s deck. The ship caught a better wind and leaped over waves. They were flying now. Despite all its masts and sails, the *Heart's Revenge* was bigger, less maneuverable, less able to tack into winds and steer around the maze of islands. The *Diana* should have pulled ahead. They should have been able to outrun Blane.

But his ship kept coming closer.

Jill gripped one of the shroud lines and lowered herself hand over hand, balancing with her feet, fast and sure, not even thinking of it, so much more confident than she had been those first days. Almost like this was home.

"Captain!" she called, running to the helm. "He's gaining!"

"Never!" Abe said. "Not in that lumbering monster!"

Cooper went to the side and looked through the spyglass. She studied the view for a long moment, and when she turned back to the helm, her expression was thoughtful. "Blane's never played by the same rules as the rest of us. He expects to chase us down and have his way with us like one of his port whores. That's it, then. We'll have to do what he doesn't expect." She had a gleam in her eyes when she turned back to the deck. "Tennant!" she shouted.

"Not yet!" he called back. Jill wanted to scream.

"You've no more time, lad!" she said. "He wants a fight,

we'll ram it down his throat. Tadpole, you still up for it?"

"Aye," Jill breathed.

"We're not going to wait for him, we're going to put our-selves in his lap before he knows we're coming and take the wind from him," the captain said. "Man the cannons! Not you, Tennant."

The thunder and chaos of a ship preparing for battle began.

Even with the sword ready, Jill wouldn't have anything to do until the real battle began. In order to fight Blane, the ships would have to draw up alongside each other. She'd have to board the *Heart's Revenge*. With all the cannon fire and fighting, she might not ever reach Blane to fight him.

She climbed back into the rigging to take up the watch again as the battle approached.

"Hoist the colors!"

There was Henry, running the black flag on its line up the mainmast. The skull on it seemed to grin.

"And ready the cannons!"

From on high, Jill looked back at the *Heart's Revenge*. It had seemed to stall, but that may have only been because the *Diana* had changed direction and the two ships were now circling each other, keeping their distance. The shore of the distant island slipped by, showing that they really were moving.

Abe shouted into the rigging; Jill barely heard him. It was newly learned habits that told her what to do to put the sails in place. The ship heeled and turned, leaving off tacking and putting the wind full behind it. The *Diana* jumped and lurched, spray flying up past the hull and into the rigging as if the ship itself were eager.

Cooper was steering them into place for a broadside. They only needed to get within range. The slots in the sides opened; the cannons rolled forward.

The *Heart's Revenge*'s cannons were more powerful, with a longer range, and they fired first. But the *Diana* had stayed pointed toward the enemy, offering a slender profile. The shots hit wide and splashed into the water. Abe called orders, spun the wheel, the *Diana* heaved over, and Cooper gave the order to fire. While the *Heart's Revenge* reloaded, the *Diana* sailed within her own range. Explosions roared, and the air filled with the smoke of burned powder.

Jill was helpless. She could only wait and hope that the *Diana* wasn't destroyed before they got close enough to board. That was Cooper's plan, she could see: Dodge cannon fire. Get within range. Make boarding the only possibility. Ram the fight down Blane's throat.

"Captain, it's done!" That was Tennant's cry. Jill raced down the lines to the deck, coughing through the smoke.

On deck, she found Cooper and Tennant standing

together. Tennant held a now-whole sword in both hands. Even amidst the smoke from the cannons, it shone silver and powerful. The blacksmith set it in the captain's waiting hands. She looked it up and down, studying it, smiling faintly. "The red in it's gone, do you see that?"

She was right; the bloody sheen had disappeared. Maybe they'd destroyed the curse, claimed the sword for their own.

"You've done a very fine job," Cooper said.

"I shouldn't have been able to do it all," Tennant said. "I didn't have the right heat, the right tools—but it's like it wanted to be whole again. It wanted to be mended."

"Blood magic," the captain whispered.

Jill would hold this newly made sword and know how to get home—she knew it. "Captain," Jill said, sounding a little too desperate.

Cooper frowned; her hand moved to the grip, tightened. Thinking of the past, perhaps. Of what she could do with the power of the sword—of taking her revenge on Blane. And Jill didn't think she could blame Cooper if the captain decided to take on Blane herself, whether or not Jill lost her way home.

But the moment passed, and Captain Cooper held the sword, grip first, to Jill. "We're going to need every blade we have, won't we?"

Jill took the weapon, one hand on the hilt, other hand

careful of the sharpened edge. She couldn't find where the break had been. The blade was healed, extending long and unbroken to a deadly point. The engravings were gone, hammered clean by Tennant's work. The sword was smooth, fresh, reborn. It sat heavy in her hands, but balanced. Dangerous. Her arm felt powerful, holding it—like the tingle she'd felt when she first found the shard, but more. She couldn't tell if the power came from the blade, or from the knowledge that she held an extraordinary sword.

But the whisper of power remained a whisper, and the only message she got from it—Blane had to be defeated.

"Thank you," she said to Tennant, who nodded.

The ships approached each other, becoming shrouded in the clouds of smoke now hanging over the water.

Jill lost track of the explosions; she could no longer differentiate between one blast of cannon fire and the next, and couldn't tell if a given explosion was the *Diana's* cannons or Blane's ship's. The ship was taking damage, splinters of wood flying, sails ripping, the shrouds playing free after being torn loose. The masts creaked and swayed. Jill kept waiting for the ship to fall apart around her. It didn't.

The *Diana* couldn't fire cannons from this position. Speed was their only weapon now—in moments, the *Heart's Revenge* wouldn't be able to fire, either, because their range would be off. They'd overshoot. Jill recognized the tactic from fencing: Get inside your opponent's reach, making their offense useless, then strike. But Cooper's ship had to move quickly, before their enemy could find the range again.

Abe took up the command. "All hands! All hands! Let the sheets out!"

Then Captain Cooper's voice came through during a heartbeat of calm. "We're comin' up on them, lads! Ready arms!"

Amidst the smoke and splinters, then, the dozen or so crew above decks swarmed to the rigging. Jill took her place at the fore mainsail. She looked out, trying to see the *Heart's Revenge* through the haze. The ship heeled as Abe turned her hard to starboard. Jill had become used to the rolling lurch of a ship making a turn like this, and balanced on loose knees, ready to haul line. Henry had the same position opposite her, on the port side, grinning, like always.

The schooner was now headed directly toward the *Heart's Revenge*.

Cooper had picked the right moment in the two ships' circling. Because the *Diana* had the wind behind her, she had the speed. Blane's ship was sluggish to react.

At the captain's command, most of the crew had gathered on the deck with an array of weapons: muskets, braces of pistols crossed over their chests, some combination of swords and daggers in both hands, and then spears and pikes—they'd probably started out as boat hooks.

Jill felt Blane's sword sing. She turned it in her hand, testing a movement, a disengage and attack, and marveled at how well balanced it was. It didn't seem to weigh anything, as if it really was an extension of her arm. Maybe she *could* fight Blane.

The crew didn't shout, didn't stand at the rail, carrying on in order to intimidate the other crew. There was no point to that. This time, they stood silent and ready.

Shouting carried from the deck of the other ship— maneuvering orders, commands to adjust the sails. Calls to arms, to battle.

The *Diana* was going to ram the other ship head on, out of reach of cannon fire. Jill couldn't believe it, but what else could happen? The ship sailed forward, strong and sure, her bowsprit leading like a sword. The *Heart's Revenge* seemed to bob, stationary, trying to turn but having no wind to move her.

"Hard to starboard! Hard over!" Cooper shouted at the last minute, and the ship lurched, turning in as sharp an arc as Jill had yet seen. When the *Diana* did collide with the *Heart's Revenge*, instead of shattering into her hull, piercing her with her bowsprit and becoming hopelessly tangled, the two ships came together bow to bow, hulls pressing together. Wood groaned.

The *Diana* seemed tiny next to Blane's three-masted monster of a ship. The other ship's deck rose above the *Diana*'s to the height of a person. A mass of the other crew crowded to the edge, shouting in fury. Then they started jumping over.

The crew of the *Diana* backed away and let them come; they'd have been cut down if they'd tried to throw ropes up and climb aboard the *Heart's Revenge*. So the enemy crew piled down to the deck of the *Diana*, where the *Diana*'s crew met them head-on.

The madness had a method to it: Those with muskets and pistols took up positions in the front and let loose a volley, cannon in miniature, that took out the first of those who'd boarded. That left the stragglers for the swords and daggers, while the next round of muskets and pistols came forward. Jill didn't know if there was another round after that, and there wasn't time to reload.

She fought. No time for precision here, no time for planning or elegance. Nobody was watching to admire her stance or judge her skill. She'd only win if she came through this alive. It was much more focused incentive than a medal or championship qualification.

Letting her vision go soft, she could take in action on the whole deck, at least in abstract. People moved all around; the enemy was in front, and her friends were around her.

But the enemy was trying to cut through the line. She cut back. Once the muskets and pistols had all fired, the battle became a tangle of blades.

Fencing is easy, the joke went. *You just put the pointy end in the other person.*

Jill tried. She blocked with the dagger Henry had given her and slashed with her rapier, half knowing that the slashing was distracting her enemy at best. Then the line ahead of her broke and a target presented itself.

A scroungy man with an angry snarl, broken teeth, and a chipped sword in each hand. He might even have been one of the ones who would have thrown her over the cliff back on New Providence. He was slashing at one of her crewmates, shouting, beating him down—the man only had a pair of daggers. A spent musket lay at his feet. The attacker didn't see Jill at all, right beside him.

This was how it went, then.

She thrust, stabbing him under the ribs, twisting her sword, then lunging back and out of the way. It was easier than she thought it would be—took barely any effort at all. Flesh was fragile. The blood came far too easily. She didn't have time to think of it.

Screeching, he arched his back, flailing at nothing. Blood poured out, turning his unwashed tunic red. She slashed at his arm; he dropped the sword. The *Diana* crewman lunged next, dagger straight out, and put it in the man's gut. He, too, made a wrenching move and turned away, keeping hold of the weapon—you didn't want to lose your weapon here. The attacker doubled over, groaning wretchedly. He wasn't dead, but he was done.

The man she'd helped—Matthews—nodded at her and plunged back in the fight.

A sheen of blood marred the upper third of Blane's rapier, fresh and glaring.

A mass battle changed more quickly, was more frenetic, than a duel. Jill decided she liked dueling better. Here, people fought in groups, three and four of them, watching each other's backs. A crowd of them would bunch together, then suddenly the area where they'd been would clear as the groups split and reformed somewhere else, and so the fighting ranged all over the ship. Jill lunged and slashed at anyone who approached. She did it more to keep the space around her clear than she did to hurt or kill anyone. If she could just keep a clear space around herself, she'd be safe.

Then, for a brief moment, no one else came for her. The battle hadn't stopped; crashing weapons and shouted curses still dominated, drowning even the splash of waves against hulls and the rippling of sails. Jill came to rest against the foremast, leaning against the stout pole to catch her breath.

Across the ship, she caught sight of Captain Cooper.

The captain was staring toward the deck of the *Heart's Revenge* with murder in the set of her jaw. The woman sheathed her sword.

Captain Cooper hauled herself up the shroud, as skilled and nimble as any of her crew, and hacked at a line, one of the ropes hanging off the yard of the mainsail. Then she climbed it, pushed off the mast, and swung to the deck of the *Heart's Revenge*. She actually swung—just like in the movies, after all.

When the captain reached the enemy's deck, she drew her sword and looked around, urgent. She was on the hunt and out for blood.

Jill put her sword in its hanger and dagger in her belt and followed.

She climbed the shrouds to reach the level of the other deck and hesitated. It must have been ten feet from here to there—a long space, with a fall on hard wood when she missed. Captain Cooper had made it look easy, had known exactly which rope to slice to carry her over the space. Jill looked around, stricken, unable to figure out the trick of it. She could see it now: She'd try to swing over and end up hanging there like a caught fish, swinging crazily and wondering how to get down.

Jill didn't want to mess with it. She jumped.

Arms out, she grabbed for the side of Blane's ship, hooked

her elbows over, which left her feet dangling. But she didn't fall. Hoping no one decided to attack her while she flailed, she pulled herself up, swinging and hooking her leg over and finally rolling onto the deck of the *Heart's Revenge*.

She glanced below, to the deck of the *Diana*. The battle there was a mob, a tangle of bodies, weapons, shouting, and blood. She'd never get the blood off the deck.

But she was on enemy territory now. Pressing her back to the side, she took in the deck of the *Heart's Revenge*.

There in the center, swords drawn, Marjory Cooper and Edmund Blane circled each other. A few of Blane's crew remained on the ship, but they held back, watching with a mix of anticipation and fear—jaws clenched, hands on hilts, but swords left in hangers. Like they wanted to help Blane, but they didn't dare. They didn't dare cross Cooper.

Jill drew her sword. Blane's sword; hers now that it was whole. Sunlight gleamed along its length and turned it to silver.

Blane's men saw it, recognized it, and began to whisper among themselves. She moved forward, and Blane's crew backed away—calmly enough, but with trepidation in their gazes. Jill didn't think she was all that scary—but if they saw her as the apprentice of Captain Marjory Cooper, the fearsome pirate queen? And if they feared Blane's sword? Maybe she was scarier than she thought. That made her straighten and put a wicked curl in her lips.

Then, his attention drawn by the commotion, Blane saw her. He glanced at Cooper and chuckled.

"What have you done, Marjory? Mended the rapier?"

"Never you mind, you bastard. Fight me, will you!"

But Blane circled around Cooper, creeping past her in order to get closer to Jill. "No," he murmured. "I'm going to take back what's mine. Perhaps a second sacrifice would make me even more powerful."

Jill squeezed her hand around the hilt, rearranging her grip. She could fight him. This was what she'd come here to do.

"Keep away from her," Cooper said, and put herself between Blane and Jill. "She's just a child. Be a man and fight *me*!"

No, Jill wanted to shout. They'd agreed on it. This was her fight—she would face Blane. But that wasn't what Cooper had in mind. The captain of the *Diana* launched an attack, sword raised, lunging at Blane as she roared in anger. Blane smoothly raised his sword to parry and knocked the attack out of the way.

Cooper didn't stop. She swung the blade around for another attack, hunting for the next opening, pressing as she did so that Blane had to scurry backward to maintain distance between them. She had him on the defensive, delivering blow after blow. Jill had to focus to work out all the movements. But none of the attacks got through. Blane repelled them all. In her fury, Cooper was less careful of her own defense.

Blane sidestepped, removing himself from her line of attack and countering with his own thrust at her face. She retreated a wide step, nearly falling into a couple of watching crewmen who scrambled out of the way. This broke her rhythm. Now Blane had the advantage. Now he was the one who pressed.

Captain Cooper swung out of the corner that Blane was trying to trap her in and ranged back to the center of the deck. Blades struck in earnest now, steel smacking and scraping against steel. Cooper met each of Blane's attacks with a strong parry and each time delivered a counterattack. But Blane never let an opening stay open for long. They were both good, really good. Jill could have just watched them, in awe of their skill and effort. It was because they fought for blood. They fought with everything they had. That made the fight different. Made it terrifying.

Sweat soaked Cooper's long hair, making it stick to her cheeks and back; her shirt grew damp with it. Blane's expression was grim, his face flushed. He still wore his coat and must have been roasting in it; at one point he rubbed the sleeve across his face and the velvet came away dark with sweat. But their movements never slowed, their intensity never faded. By her snarl, Cooper clearly wanted to kill him. By his grimness, Blane clearly wasn't about to let her.

Noises thumped on the side of the *Heart's Revenge*—hooks coming over the side and people climbing up the ropes attached to them. Jill leaned over, uncertain, fearful—were they Blane's crew, returning after a slaughter, or Cooper's crew, victorious? If the *Heart's Revenge* crew had slaughtered the crew of the *Diana*, they might as well let Blane win the duel—they were all dead then anyway.

It was Henry who appeared over the side of the *Heart's Revenge* first. He had blood smeared across one cheek.

He saw Jill and grinned. "What's going—" But he saw, and his mouth opened in shock.

Apart from the constant background noises of waves and wind always present on a ship at sea, they only heard the beat of boot steps on the deck as Cooper and Blane moved back and forth, their gasps for breath and huffs of effort. The sounds of fighting had faded, and even the fog of gunpowder had blown away. Everyone else just watched.

There came a hiccup in the rhythm of swords crossing and bodies moving. The fighters closed for what seemed just a moment, their blades caught against each other as the two crashed together in a failed attack. With a cry of rage Blane disentangled himself with a slash of his blade. Cooper shouted back, right in his face, and her own weapon turned.

Jill thought it was done, that it was all over for him. But it was Captain Cooper who fell away, a slash of red marring her side.

Shouts of anger cried out from the side of the ship. The *Diana*'s crew, reacting. Some of them ran forward to reach their captain—Henry, Abe, Tennant. The members of Blane's crew remaining on deck surged, growling, weapons out, ready to do battle.

Jill ran forward, screaming her own cry of battle. She swept Blane's rapier around her, defending a space.

"Get back!" she shouted, putting herself between Blane's men and Captain Cooper. "Get away, all of you!"

Jill spared a glance back, dreading what she would see. But Cooper was alive. A grimace creased her face, and she snarled at her crewmen. "I'm fine, it's only a cut, let go of me!" But her voice was strained, and she was hugging her arms around her middle, holding in a flow of blood.

"Henry! Get that surgeon up here! Go now!" Abe shouted. Henry jumped back to the *Diana* and ran below-decks.

Abe and Tennant finished dragging Cooper out of the way, toward the side and back toward the *Diana*. Matthews guarded their escape with a pair of pistols. Jill kept herself in front of Blane.

Edmund Blane was using a handkerchief to wipe blood off his sword. He stepped slowly around her; she moved to keep him in view. Holding her sword at him, she stared at him down its length. The tip of the sword shook because her arm was trembling.

"How do you like it? It's got a good weight to it, doesn't it?" he said casually, unconcerned. "Now that you've got it in one piece, do you know what to do with it?"

She remained silent, repeating old fencing lessons in her mind. Point your toe, keep your knees bent, keep the blade on line, never attack on a bent arm. Advance, retreat, lunge, recover. She liked to think she knew what to do with a rapier.

"I'll make a bargain with you," Blane said, stuffing the bloodied handkerchief up one sleeve. He kept his rapier out and ready. "Give me my sword, and the *Diana* and all her crew can go free. You can tend to Marjory—it isn't a deep wound, I'll wager. If you can stop the bleeding, she should live. You can all live—if you give me my sword." He spoke this loud enough to carry to the crew of the *Diana* who were watching.

Jill didn't know what to do. Her first impulse, her first instinct, was to toss the sword at his feet and run back to her friends. This shocked her. That shouldn't have been what she wanted to do at all. After everything she'd done to get it, after all the worry she'd spent over it, she'd get rid of it so easily, without a fight? She'd give up her way home without a fight? And she realized if she had to choose between going home and the lives of her friends, she couldn't. If she could save them, she had to.

She looked over her shoulder. Cooper was propped against the side. Abe was with her, and Emory had arrived. The surgeon was packing a bandage into the wound at her side. Henry and Tennant stood guard, even though Tennant only had a dagger with him. They were all watching her.

Marjory Cooper shook her head. *No, don't do it.* And Henry shook his head. Abe smiled. She knew they were right because Blane would never keep his word. They would all back her up, whatever happened.

Jill looked at Edmund Blane and shook her head.

His lip curled in a sneer. Then he struck.

It was a textbook feint—straight arm, forward thrust. He expected to catch her off guard, expected her to parry wide, flailing, leaving her defenseless while he disengaged to another line of attack and skewered her. Her fencer's brain mapped it out a quarter of a second before it happened because she'd seen it before, she'd practiced against a move like that a million times. And lately, she'd been practicing with pirates. When he attacked, she didn't have to stand there waiting for him.

She sidestepped out of his way and beat his blade off line, giving him nothing to counterattack against and no opening. But he was fast and smart and recovered quickly, attacking again.

She let her fears go, her anxieties fade, bringing all her attention to the flashing steel before her. Her body knew what to do, and the rapier fit neatly in her hand, comfortable and deadly. The world focused in on his blade and her own, and how the two interacted. He didn't let her rest; every moment was taken up with attack and counterattack, parries and ripostes, trying to hit while avoiding getting hit herself. Sweat gathered in her hair and trickled down her back, under her shirt. An annoyance she could do nothing about, it made her aware of her whole body and how close the edged steel was coming to it.

He flicked his weapon at her, she parried—and was striking at an opening before her higher brain even knew it was there. A length of forearm behind his glove. She thrust at it, heard ripping as the point caught the shirt, felt resistance of flesh. He shouted, and she scurried back as his sword swung toward her again.

Blood stained the sleeve of his right arm. Not a lot. But enough to show the man was mortal.

And she remained standing, sword in her hand, watching him. So it would take more than a little blood for the power of the sword to send her home. They'd have to finish this, and she frowned, daunted.

His fury was controlled as he came at her again, his attacks even more powerful, so that each parry she made rattled her arm. Her muscles were turning to rubber. If he was at all tired after fighting Cooper, he hid it well.

On the other hand, Jill wasn't sure how much longer she could keep this up. In competition, a tournament might last all day, but a single bout might last only a few minutes. Even with dozens of bouts in a day, she'd have lots of rests in between. She was missing the rests, now. She only wanted a chance to catch her breath. But she had to keep going. If she slowed, Blane would see it and cut her down.

Her heart was beating in her throat, her temples were pounding. If she could only cut him again, and then a dozen more times—

With a renewed bout of strength, he pressed, and she retreated, hoping for a spare breath and a chance to recover. She felt the cut on her left arm without seeing exactly how he had made it—he growled, frowning, which made her think that he'd missed and meant to hit something more vital. The stinging wound seemed distant.

Instead of pulling back a moment and reassessing—as

she had done after she struck him—he drove even harder. She couldn't even counter now, only move her sword in a constant parry and hope her defensive wall was enough to keep him out. She jumped sideways, hoping to duck out from under his onslaught, but he stayed right with her.

All she needed was an opening, a moment when he let his guard down, a chance for her to strike. But then, that was all he needed, too.

She gathered another burst of strength, hoping to make one last attack, a last concerted exchange that would give her the opening she needed and finish this. She beat his blade, attacked. He made a hurried retreat, and she thought, *This is it.*

Then Blane fell.

His feet slipped out from under him and he toppled like a cartoon character. *But I didn't do anything,* came Jill's first thought.

Then she saw the hook and rope tangled around his legs. And Henry crouched nearby, holding the other end of the line.

Jill marched forward and lay the point of her rapier on Blane's neck, like it was the most natural, normal thing to do.

The captain of the *Heart's Revenge* had been struggling to sit up, but confronted by Jill's steel he simply lay there, breathing hard, sweating, craning his head up to try to see her without impaling himself. His expression was an ugly sneer. Jill didn't dare look away from him.

"Finish him off!" Henry called.

She knew what he meant—a slice across his throat, a stab through his neck and spinal cord. An ugly, messy death. He'd twitch on her sword like a bug on a pin. It'd be easy to do, with him lying there. The sword itself seemed to yearn toward him, eager to slice into him. She felt the power of it in her fingers, wrist, and arm. And if she was right, this would send her home—feed the sword Blane's life in exchange for the child's life he'd taken with it. It ought to be easy, with so much at stake.

And she realized she couldn't. Not even to send herself home.

"You cheated," Jill said to Henry.

"Course I did, you weren't going to beat him," he said.

Henry didn't know that. Anything could have happened. That last attack might have worked. But part of her was just as glad not to have to find out. Blane was beaten, and it didn't matter who gave the final blow.

"I'm not going to kill dead a man who's flat on his back," Jill said. "That's the kind of thing *he* would do."

"A woman of honor," Blane said with contempt. "Nice."

Yes, she thought. *I am.*

"Drop your sword," she said, flicking the point against his skin. It scraped but didn't cut. But just a little more pressure . . .

Blane let go of his weapon. Jill kicked it away, and it rattled across the wooden deck.

Her arm became very tired, then. The sword she held no longer called out for blood, no longer surged with power. It was just a weight of steel. Well-made, beautiful steel. But nothing more.

Mostly, then, it was done. With their captain defeated, Blane's men turned docile. They sat by the gunwales and didn't make trouble. They'd been loyal to Blane's power, which was gone now. The crew of the *Diana* had defeated the boarding party. The cannons were silent.

Captain Cooper got to her feet, aided by Abe and the doctor. But she walked over to Jill under her own power, limping, hand pressed to her side over the bandage wrapped around her middle.

"Come to gloat then, Marjory?" Blane said, hateful as ever.

"Henry," she said softly. "Tie the bastard up. Good and tight."

Henry did, tying Blane's hands and feet with yards of rope, tying another loop around the pirate's neck so if he tried to move too much he'd strangle himself.

Finally, Jill could lower the rapier. It was just a sword now. It had defeated its master, tasted Blane's blood. Any mysticism she'd felt from it, any power it had given her, seemed to have dissipated. She felt weak, like she wanted to melt. Her muscles were loose, exhausted.

Captain Cooper stood beside her, in front of Blane, now trussed and lying by the forecastle of the ship.

"Are you all right, Tadpole?" she said.

"Aren't I a frog yet?"

Cooper chuckled and squeezed Jill's shoulder. Jill sighed. "I couldn't kill him. Was that wrong?"

"No. It's never wrong, that's what the preachers say. But I think it means you don't really belong out here."

That was what Jill had known all along.

"On the other hand, a quick death's too good for him, isn't it? I'd like to see him hang in a gibbet," she said. Jill just stared.

"Ahoy! Ship ahoy!" The call came from the *Diana*. No lookout had been posted during the battle, but one of the sailors leaned over the prow of the smaller ship and shouted. Everyone looked.

Beyond the spit of shore that marked the end of the island, an incongruous shape emerged, a bright glint against the water. Jill squinted, trying to bring the spot into focus, wishing for the captain's spyglass. Then the spot moved, gliding upon the water, coming into full view. Another ship, three-masted, under full sail, moving fast. A spot of color flashed amidst the sails—the red and white of the British navy.

"It's the bloody navy, just what we need right now," Cooper muttered. She marched to Emory and grabbed his collar, curling it in her fist—then wincing and pressing a hand to her bandaged side. But her voice was no less fierce. "One of your friends, then?"

Emory glanced out at the navy ship, circling the area like a predator.

"She's the HMS *Ivy*. I believe she's been tracking you since Jamaica."

"With your help?"

Emory wouldn't look at her. "I imagine they were waiting for the battle to end."

"So they could sail in pretty as birds to clean up the scraps? I ought to hang you from the bowsprit and ram you through their hull!"

"Captain," Emory said. "Let me signal them. I'm sure we can work out a deal. The reward for Blane is considerable—"

"I don't trust you. You're just trying to find a way off this boat and sell us all out besides."

"I can't deny it."

Cooper snarled at him.

"Captain!" Abe called. "Speaking of gibbets, maybe we should let the English sharks have him?"

Emory brightened for the first time since Jill had seen him. He made a quick nod. "That sounds very agreeable. I can raise flags to signal the *Ivy* and have them come alongside—"

The captain shook her head. "We're not talking about you, we're talking about Blane."

"Captain, please, I won't say a word against you—"

"No." Cooper turned to her quartermaster. "Abe. How'd you like your own ship?"

Abe glanced over the deck of the *Heart's Revenge*, her masts and sails the worse for wear after the battle but still whole, still seaworthy. If possible, his grin grew wider. "I think that would be a very fine thing. But I think she'll need a new name."

Cooper regarded the captured ship, squinting into the sun, thoughtfully pursing her lips. "Aye, I think you're right. You have a thought?"

"I do," he said. "*Heart's Ease*. It's a good name—and it will drive Blane mad."

Cooper addressed Blane's surviving crew who'd been gathered, battered and bleeding, to face their conqueror. "All right, you scurvy lot. You've got a choice. You keep your old places on your old ship with one of my crew as your captain, you sign my articles and forget all the tripe that bugger fed you—you do all that, you'll be free as you ever were on these waters. Or you can follow your captain into irons and the admiralty's prison."

All of Blane's men agreed to become part of a new crew.

Cooper turned to the gunnery mate next. "Tennant? Prepare a boat for our friends so we can deliver our package properly."

"Aye, sir!"

"The rest of you—get to your posts and ready to make sail, unless you want to hang in a gibbet tomorrow!" Abe repeated the command, and the crews of two ships rushed to action.

Captain Cooper and most of her crew made their way back to her own ship. The captain was weakened, everyone could see it. Her face was pale and she moved slowly. But her attitude remained intact. She glared and shouted and berated her crew, same as always, which made the world feel like all was well.

"Is she going to be all right?" Jill asked Emory when she had a chance, back on the deck of the *Diana*.

"She needs to rest," he said. "But yes, I think she will be. Curse her, I've got to get off this ship." He gazed at the navy ship as if he was considering swimming for it.

A familiar boom thudded across the water; smoke rose from the *Ivy's* side—they'd fired a cannon. It seemed to be just a warning shot—nothing was hit. But if the *Diana* was going to run, they'd have to do it soon.

"You don't need to leave," Emory said. "Once I've explained the situation, they'll grant you amnesty—"

"What exactly will you explain to them?" Cooper said. "That you've captured one infamous pirate captain—or two?"

The rowboat was ready. Overhead, sails were rippling, tugging at masts, and the *Diana* lurched like a dog at a leash.

"It's time," Cooper said. "Put Blane over and we'll leave him for His Majesty's friends."

"What about the reward money?" Emory said. "You could—"

"We've got Blane's ship, and that's reward enough for us."

Blane, secured by ropes and burdened by chains—Abe had found the chains they'd broken off the Africans and used them to make him doubly secured—was dragged to the side and lowered over, like so much cargo. At the bottom of the boat he thrashed against his bindings, which caused the little boat to rock until ocean water sloshed over the sides.

"I curse you, Marjory Cooper!" he shouted at her. "With

all my blood and spit I curse you!"

"No less than I expected, love!" she hollered back at him. Then she turned to the surgeon one more time. "Mr. Emory, your turn. You can explain to the navy all you want."

"Pardon me?"

"I'm sick of you. You want to talk to the navy so badly, you go with Blane and talk to them. Collect the reward money yourself if you want it. Unless you'd rather stay here?"

The surgeon smiled wryly. "Aye, sir. I mean, no. That is—as you wish, as always."

Without further argument, he took hold of the line that had been used to lower Blane. Then he turned to Jill, who was leaning on the nearby shrouds, watching the proceedings like a regular sailor.

"Miss Jill? How's your arm? Is it hot to the touch?"

Jill checked the stitched-up wound on her left arm. It was healing, pink flesh bound up with dark threads. It itched and was tender when she touched it, but it wasn't hot, it didn't hurt.

"No," she said. "It's all right, I think. Thank you."

"Good. And—I meant what I said. If you want to come with me, I can get you a pardon and take you away from here. Take you back to wherever you came from."

But he couldn't. He wouldn't understand the explanation. More so, because there was more than that reason not to go with him. He couldn't take her home. And she didn't want to leave Captain Cooper and Henry and the rest to go with him.

"Thank you, but no," she said. "I'll be all right here."

Emory nodded to her, then went over the side. When he reached the rowboat, Tennant cut it loose from the *Diana*. By then, the schooner was already under sail. Canvas filled with wind on both ships. Within moments, sailing side by side, a tiny fleet of their own, they left the rowboat behind.

More explosions boomed; more cannon fire from the *Ivy*. This time, water splashed nearby—they were finding the range.

Cooper and her crew, and Abe and his, watched as the navy ship sent out launches of its own after the rowboat that had been set adrift, until they were too far away and the boats were no more than specks. The *Ivy* stopped firing, and seemed more interested in what had been left behind.

"Best of luck to them," Cooper said lightly. The air seemed brighter now that Blane was gone.

Jill sat down on the deck, back to the gunwale on the port side, watching it all with a sense of calm, of satisfaction that was strange to her. She was exhausted. She'd won, she supposed. She may not have struck down Blane, she may not have fenced brilliantly with dazzling skill. Nevertheless, she felt like she'd won. She should be happy. All was right with the world, which at the moment was entirely encompassed by this little ship, her crew, and her captain.

But she still didn't know how to get home.

A shadow fell across her; Henry stood over her, scowling, arms crossed.

"That was bloody stupid," he said. "Bloodiest stupid thing I ever saw. You should have run him through. Killed him dead. It's what he deserved, an' he'd a done the same to you without thinking."

Maybe that was the sense of calm that had settled heavily into her limbs, making her blood flow thickly, warmly: relief that she was alive. She'd survived. She'd never felt so relieved after a fencing bout—those were just for points, after all. This was *brilliant*.

Not that she ever wanted to fight for her life again. She'd be happy enough to go back to the strip and just have fun. After today, competitive fencing couldn't be anything but fun.

She smiled up at Henry, which must have infuriated him. "It's okay. It's all okay. I did exactly the right thing."

"You're loony is what. Heat's got to you." He slumped to the deck beside her and studied her. "You could have been killed, Jill. Then what would I have done?"

"Aren't you the one who's always saying we're all going to die young? Then what does it matter?"

"That's not what I meant," he said.

She took his hand, squeezed it. He continued to look grim.

"All right, you stinking loafers, get off your bums, we've a schooner to clean up, and we'll be following Abe to make sure he's set to right with his crew. Lots of work and not many hours of light left, so move!"

Jill and Henry pulled each other to their feet and scrambled to follow orders.

Cannonballs had taken chunks out of the *Diana*'s mainmast, which needed to be shored up. Decks were split, pocked with musket shot, and spattered with blood. Lines had broken, rigging swung loose, tackle was lost, and some of the sails hung in useless tatters. Crewmembers climbed to bring down the damaged pieces. Jill was one of those who sat on deck, mending sail, splicing rope, knotting and reknotting until her hands grew raw and blistered.

The *Heart's Ease* sailed several hundred feet larboard of the *Diana*. They could send supplies back and forth and help each other with repairs. And Cooper could keep an eye on Blane's old crew. But they actually seemed relieved to have Blane gone.

By dusk, much of the work was done. Food and rum came out, and the party began.

Henry brought Jill a drink and sat with her. Jill could

drink watered rum now without choking on it. She'd gotten used to the burn of it. Still, she'd have done just about anything for a cold soda right then. She leaned on the side, watching the celebration as the fiddles and drums came out and the singing and dancing started. She might have fought in a real sword fight, she might be able to climb the rigging like a monkey, like any seasoned sailor, and she could drink rum. But could she stay here? Could she be happy? She didn't know much about the history, but she knew where Marjory Cooper, Henry, and all the crew were likely to end up: killed in a battle, taken down by cannon fire or musket shot, sunk and drowned; or captured and dragged to Port Royal, to be hanged and left in a cage for crows.

And they'd all tell her that they'd be proud and happy to meet such an end.

This time, it was Captain Cooper who blocked the light from the lanterns that blazed across the deck, when she came up and leaned on the side next to Jill and regarded the scene.

"That sword should go back to the sea. The whole thing this time. Send it to the bottom and be done with it," Cooper said. She left the command behind the statement unspoken: that if Jill didn't throw the thing over, Cooper would take it from her and do it.

She was right, Jill thought. Maybe Blane was gone,

maybe the sword wasn't dangerous without him. But why take the chance? Then she had another thought: The shard on its own had been her key here, and she was sure the whole sword was her key home, she just wasn't sure how. How to find the way home when she'd come here by accident, and no one understood the magic of it, not even Blane?

But now, she thought she had an idea. Ruby slippers.

"What if it comes back again? What if someone like Blane finds it?" Jill held her breath a moment, thinking, hoping the faint idea didn't fade. She straightened, gripping the hilt, tilting it so it flickered in the lantern light. If it didn't work, she could swim. But she had a feeling.

"No one'll find it," Henry said. "The sea keeps its own."

Except for me, Jill thought.

The captain stood, tossing back a drink from her flask. "Let's do it and have done with it, then toast it to hell. You do the honors, Tadpole?"

Jill held the rapier close, point down and to her side. "Okay."

She looked around one more time. Caught a few of her crewmate's gazes—Tennant, Matthews, Bessie, Jane. They smiled at her, raising their mugs to her. She wished she could say good-bye to Abe. Beside her, Henry smiled, then frowned, because he guessed what she was thinking. She touched his arm.

She wouldn't stay to watch them all die young, as pirates did.

Jill sat on the rail, swung a leg over, and remained astride it for a moment, looking over the place that had been her home for the last few weeks. She still wasn't sure she understood this life. She was pretty sure it would all turn out to be a dream. Strange, though, how the smell of pitch, canvas, and salt water had become so comforting.

"Jill, no, have you gone barmy?" Henry reached for her.

"Henry, what're you on about?" Cooper said. "Tadpole? Jill?"

They must have seen the farewell in her expression.

"Thank you," she said to them both.

She swung her other leg over and took only a brief look down to the black water and waves chopping against *Diana*'s hull. Then she slid off, clutching the sword to her chest with both hands.

The water was cold and shocked the breath out of her; she thought she'd been ready, but she flailed, kicking and swinging with her arms, hoping to find the surface. Her lungs burned, her chest tightened. But she kept a fierce grip on the sword. She couldn't let it go.

For a terrible moment, she wondered if she wasn't swimming up but down. She couldn't see anything and felt herself tossed by waves. Then, the world turned bright. Sunlight.

The water went from black to turquoise. Her face broke the surface and she gasped, swallowing air like a fish gulps water. Hands grabbed her, just like they had before. There were people clinging to her, shouting.

"Oh my God, is she okay? Is she all right?"

Jill recognized her mother's voice.

Then she was hanging over the side of a modern fiberglass boat with a big motor, the kind that ferried tourists around the Bahamas. The kind of boat she'd fallen out of at the start. The sun was high in the sky, just as it had been, the storm clouds were off in the distance, but not threatening. Her father and the tour guide held her, gripping her shirt and arms, making sure she didn't slide back into the water. The guide also held a ring-style life preserver, and a couple more of the boat tour people stood to the side. The boat's engine grumbled, keeping them steady and in one place.

Jill gasped for breath, but she wanted to laugh. She was in her clamdiggers and tank top, just like before. Everything was just like before, like none of it had happened. Like she'd fallen overboard and been fished out in her own world, her own time, in a matter of seconds. Except that her other arm, the one not hooked over the side of the boat, still held Edmund Blane's sword.

She swung her leg over to climb fully aboard. Everyone looked so scared. Her father hugged her and pulled her up—and didn't let her go. She hugged him back, one-armed, tight as she could. She was home.

"Jill, are you all right? What happened? Are you hurt?" Dad said, over and over. She'd never heard him sound so worried.

Before she could answer, her brother pointed at her and exclaimed. "Jeez, where'd you get that?"

Everyone stared as Jill pulled away from her father's grip and regarded the weapon in her hand. It was definitely Edmund Blane's, with the same sleek blade and graceful swept hilt. But the whole thing was covered with rust—rough, dark black, soaked with slime and seawater. It was ancient, corroded; it might have been sitting on the ocean floor for, oh—three hundred years?

And how did she explain it all? How did she tell them what had happened to her? They'd never believe it, any more than Cooper's crew would believe where she'd come from. They'd think she was crazy. They'd check her for a head injury. And maybe they'd be right to think she was crazy. Surely it couldn't have happened.

But she remembered it so clearly. All of it. The smell of the *Diana*, the sails rippling overhead, the noise of cannon fire, battling with Edmund Blane, kissing Henry—

She could never tell them about it.

"It was on the bottom," Jill said, still catching her breath.

"I saw it and just reached for it."

She held the sword in both hands, so they all could see. Her mother and father were at her sides, and her siblings pressed closed. The rest of the tourists on the cruise gathered around wonderingly, and the grizzled tour guide studied the artifact admiringly.

"That's amazing," someone said. "How long do you think it's been down there?"

"Look how rusted it is."

"Where do you think it came from?"

"It's from a pirate ship, I bet," her brother said.

Jill glanced at her brother and hid a smile.

"I suppose we ought to take it to a museum," her mother said.

Reflexively, Jill took a tighter grip on the sword. She could see it, this piece of history sitting in a display case in a museum somewhere, right where it belonged, next to a placard explaining its date and place of origin and what it said about the seafaring world of the eighteenth-century Bahamas, locked away from people and no one watching over it once the museum closed—and Blane somehow finding a way to steal it back. She told Captain Cooper she'd keep it safe. A museum, with its guards and alarms, ought to be safe. But Jill didn't want to let it go.

"Do we have to?" Jill said, trying to explain. "I mean,

this is like my own history. I'm a fencer. The weapons I use, my épées—they evolved from this, the kind of fighting I do came from this. It's like I was meant to find it. You know? Like I fell overboard just to find this." She turned hopefully to the tour guide. If anyone would know what should legally happen to the sword, it was him.

After a moment of thought, he smiled at her. "Law of salvage, kid. As far as I'm concerned, it's yours. But let's get it in a cooler, it needs to stay in water until we can get it to someone who can do some restoration on it." He emptied out the long cooler of its ice and sodas—cold sodas. Jill almost lunged for one. But there'd be time for that soon enough. After filling the cooler with ocean water, Jill set the sword inside. It barely fit diagonally.

"Mom, Dad, it's okay if I keep this, right?"

They both had their hands on her shoulders, unwilling to let go, as if reassuring themselves that she was safe. Her mother ran a hand over her wet hair. Jill didn't mind.

"I suppose any museums we could show it to have a lot better-looking rapiers than this," her father said. "It's pretty rusted over."

"That doesn't matter," Jill said.

She started shivering, because she was still wet through, and a cool wind was blowing over the water. The kind of wind that would catch sails and drive a well-rigged schooner across the sea. One of the crew found a blanket for her, and she sat huddled in the cabin to dry off and get warm. Her parents still kept to her side. And Jill still couldn't stop smiling.

"You seem awfully happy for having almost drowned," Mom said.

Jill had to agree.

Epilogue

TOUCHÉ

This was the best summer job she could possibly have. Almost as good as sailing on a pirate ship for a little while.

Twelve girls, ages ten to twelve, lined up in front of her on the concrete basketball court in the main activities area of Camp Mountain Oak. They had their lead toes pointed, their other feet back, their knees loose, their backs straight, their arms bent as if holding épées. Jill went to each of them and adjusted their positions.

She was teaching them how to fence.

She was at the camp primarily as a counselor, but the

camp wanted someone who could also teach fencing, and that was how Jill had gotten the job.

After a half hour of exercises, of advancing and retreating across the basketball court, drilling the movements into their brains and bodies so that they'd never forget, until the girls complained that their legs hurt and their arms were sore—"That's how you know you're doing it right," Jill told them—she gathered them around in a shady spot by the main building and brought out her prize.

She'd been allowed to keep the rapier. Her parents made some phone calls to museums and found a specialist who could clean the sword. It had taken weeks of desalinization treatments to remove the corrosion, careful grinding and scrubbing to clean the metal, and a protective acrylic coating to prevent further damage. It would never have the gleam that it had when it was new, and would never again hold a razor's edge. But that was all right. Jill only ever planned on using it to tell stories.

Jill retrieved the sword, wrapped in a thick black cloth, from her locker, and revealed it in front of the girls.

Laid out on the fabric, the sword shone like a treasure. As she hoped, the girls crowded forward to get a better look, oohing and aahing.

"Is it real?" one of them asked.

"Yes," Jill said. "It's from the early eighteenth century."

"Is it a pirate sword?" another asked.

"It is, it really is. It belonged to a pirate named Edmund Blane. He was defeated in battle by another pirate, Marjory Cooper. The sword fell overboard and stayed lost in the ocean for three hundred years."

"Marjory Cooper—a girl?" one of them asked.

Jill grinned. She loved this part. "Yes. One of the fiercest pirate queens that ever sailed."

Some of them looked like they didn't believe her. Didn't believe that there were such a thing as pirate queens at all, or that women ever dressed up as men and joined armies, or did anything big and amazing and adventurous. So she pulled out her books and pictures. She'd found pictures of Mary Read and Anne Bonny that didn't look very much like they had in person, but were good enough.

In all the reading she'd done, she hadn't found anything at all about Marjory Cooper and Edmund Blane, or the *Diana* and the *Heart's Revenge*. They'd faded from history—if they'd ever been real at all.

But Jill had a scar on her left arm, three inches across her bicep, from the wound that Emory had stitched. Back at the house after the boat tour, she'd taken a shower and noticed the welt of pink, healing skin. Her mother saw it the next day and demanded to know where it had come from. Jill told her she must have gotten cut when she fell off the boat.

It was all she could do not to tell the girls about sailing aboard the *Diana* with Marjory Cooper. But she could tell them about a love of fencing, and of pirate honor.

She let each of the girls hold the sword. It was too heavy for most of them, and it wavered in their grips. Even so, with the rapier in their hands, they all stood a little taller.

AUTHOR'S NOTE

My pirates aren't movie pirates. I did a lot of research on the real pirates of the Caribbean in the early 1700s, and got a lot of ideas from that research. But my pirates aren't quite real historical pirates, either. We have lots of evidence that some women dressed as men and sailed with pirates (Anne Bonny and Mary Read are the best-known real-world examples), but no evidence that any of them were ever captains of pirate ships, at least in the Caribbean during the so-called golden age of piracy. (We do know of women pirate captains in other places, like Ireland and Southeast Asia.) And while pirates did capture slave ships traveling the route between the western coast of Africa and the Caribbean, they were more likely to sell the slaves themselves than they were to set them free, as the captain and crew of the *Diana* do. On the other hand, we also have evidence of former slaves like Abe serving on pirate crews. Grandy Nanny was a real person, one of Jamaica's national heroes, but she was active a bit later than I have her here. And while Blackbeard, Calico Jack, Stede Bonnet, Sam Bellamy, and all the pirates I name were alive at the same time, they were probably never all having a drink together in Nassau at the same time. But I couldn't resist.

We know about most of the famous pirates because they were captured or killed, witnesses interviewed, and their stories recorded in great detail for the court cases. There were hundreds of less famous pirates whom we know nothing about, simply because they were never caught. They either accepted pardons and settled into law-abiding lives, or they sailed into the sunset with their booty and retired. While we don't know of any women pirate captains in the Caribbean, I'd like to believe that's simply because if there was someone much like Captain Marjory Cooper, perhaps she was never caught.

Thanks go to Zrinka Znidarcic for answering questions about sword restoration. To Walter Jon Williams for the extensive notes on all things regarding sailing in the eighteenth century. All my errors on that topic are mine alone. To Gary Copeland and the coaches and students of Northern Colorado Fencers, whose successes in national and international competition gave me the idea for Jill in the first place. And to my fellow Defenders of the White Scarf of the Outlands, for the camaraderie and the love of rapier combat.

CHAPTER HEADINGS GLOSSARY

En garde: "On guard." The opening stance in rapier combat.

Retreat: Backward movement in rapier combat.

Disengage: An attack in which one's blade moves from one line to another under the action of an opponent's blade.

Foible: The last third of a rapier blade; the thinnest, weakest part of the blade.

Flèche: "Arrow." An attack made while leaping into a run.

Remise: The same attack continued immediately after being parried.

Redoublement: An attack continued on the opposite line immediately after being parried.

Allez: "Go." A call for rapier combatants to begin fighting.

Attack: An offensive movement in rapier combat.

Recover: Returning to an *en garde* stance after an action.

Coupé: An attack in which one's blade moves from one line to another over the action of an opponent's blade.

Beat: A quick, sharp strike against an opponent's blade.

Passé: An action in which blades cross but no touches are made.

Stop thrust: A direct attack with an extended arm against an advancing opponent.

Forte: The lowest third of a rapier blade; the strongest part of the blade.

Touché: "Touch." When the point of the rapier touches the opponent.

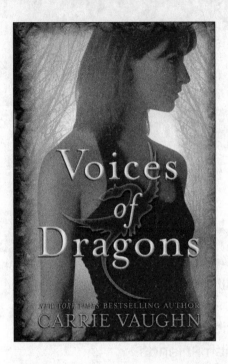